The Convenient Patsy

In This Series

That First Heady Burn
True Vermilion
The Dark Shill
A Stack of Sawbucks
The Hillside Roble
The Peroxide Pomp
The Incidental Twin
Brawl in Bardo
The Window-Shade Job
The Convenient Patsy
The Artisanal Grifter
Shrink in the Shadows
Project Chartreuse
From a Desert Playa
The Tired Canary
A Desperate Frame-up
Trail of the Blue Agave
The Saucer-Heads

The Convenient Patsy

The Convenient Patsy

George Bixley

DAGMAR
MIURA
LOS ANGELES

Published by Dagmar Miura
Los Angeles
www.dagmarmiura.com

The Convenient Patsy

This is a work of fiction. Names, characters, businesses, places, events, and incidents are either the products of the author's imagination or used in a fictitious manner. Any resemblance to actual persons, living or dead, or actual events is purely coincidental.

First published 2020

ISBN: 978-1-951130-28-2

ONE

"THIS MIGHT SOUND A little unusual to our regular listeners," the narrator said. "This week I'm taking the search to Los Angeles. No one has reported bigfoot lurking amid the palm trees, or leaving oversize footprints on the beach, but *Sasquatch Search* business is leading me there, and I'm going to need some help. At issue is an urgent research project. If you're in the City of Angels and you think you might be able to lend a hand, reach out—I'd like to hear from you."

It was a podcast Slater listened to sometimes, not because he cared about the Sasquatch, but because he found it relaxing when he was unwinding, late at night, as the voice of the imperturbable narrator pulled him out of his urban grind and into the dense and cryptic forest. Tonight he'd almost finished his full ration of bourbon, and he was only half listening, parked in his recliner in his dark apartment, looking out through the dusty window at the sky, lit by the glow of the gritty metropolis.

Slater had come out here because the guy he'd hooked up with tonight was in his bed, snoring, and it was too loud to fall sleep. He didn't mind, really. Sometimes he crashed out here anyway, and he didn't want to kick the guy out. He'd met him on a hookup app, and it felt like maybe he was homeless. The guy had taken an extremely long shower after they'd had sex, and he'd borrowed a razor. It wouldn't hurt to let him get a decent night's sleep.

Picking up his phone, he winced at the glare of the screen, and checked the date. The narrator had said Monday—that meant he would be in LA tomorrow. Slater cleared his throat and dictated an email:

> Hey, Ryan—I just listened to the latest episode of the podcast. I'm not sure what kind of research you're doing in my town, and if you're hunkering down at a library or an archive and need a book person, I can't help you. But if you're doing hands-on research, and you need real-world skills, I work as an insurance investigator, and I might be able to give you some ideas.

At the bottom he added his phone number, but then hesitated before he sent the message. Would he do this if it was eight in the morning and he was sober? Probably not. Things were different at night. Fuck it, he decided, and hit SEND.

It was late enough that the music would be getting good, and he turned on the radio, and closed his eyes, and started to doze. House music wouldn't wake the guy in his bed—he was generating a lot more noise than this with his own airway.

Sometime later Slater started awake when his phone rang. The caller ID said only "Oregon," but he knew who it was. Sitting up, he took a breath to try to sober up, and killed the radio.

"Ibáñez," he answered.

"It was good to hear from you," Ryan said, his voice familiar even though he wasn't using his measured and even narrator's intonation. "I thought I was going into the big city blind."

"What kind of research are you doing in LA?" Slater said.

"I'm looking for someone."

"What kind of someone?"

"We can get into that later. You said you're in insurance—is that like car crashes?"

"Not usually," Slater said. "Mostly I investigate fraud. Interviewing claimants in the field. The desk jockeys hire me to do things they can't handle."

"Have you ever worked a missing persons case?"

"That's definitely in my wheelhouse."

"I'm so glad to hear that. You have no idea how relieved I am just to have someone to talk to."

"You said you'd be here tomorrow?"

"My flight lands at one," Ryan said. "I'm packing right now. Can I meet up with you?"

"I'll email you my office address."

"Text it to me at this number. How far is it from the airport?"

"Which one?"

"There's more than one airport?"

"There's three or four," Slater said. "But it's probably LAX."

"Let me check my ticket." The line went quiet for a moment before Ryan spoke again. "You're right—it's LAX."

"I'm in downtown LA. From when the wheels hit the tarmac to my office is about an hour."

"So I'll see you at two."

Slater ended the call and took a second to text Ryan his street address, then got up and went to the kitchen counter to grab the fifth of bourbon and splash more of it into his tumbler. It didn't count against his limit, he told himself, because it was just a mouthful. He slammed it, and relished the burn of the heady fumes in his nose, then left the glass in the sink, but took the bottle back to his recliner and stretched out. Even with the bedroom door closed he could hear the faint sound of his hookup's rhythmic snoring.

Ryan sounded a lot more wound up tonight than he ever had on the podcast. If it was a missing-person situation, trying to find a human being in this city should be a lot easier than tracking down bigfoot in the deep forest. He tipped the bottle and took a mouthful of bourbon. This could get interesting.

TWO

N THE MORNING, WHEN he woke up, Slater
was in his bed, although he couldn't remember how he got here. There'd been a guy, he knew, but he wasn't here now. As he became more lucid, he remembered he had a meeting today. Things had been slow lately, and he hadn't expected to drum up a job in the middle of the night, but that's what he'd done.

A sound came from the main room—a dull *thump* on the carpeted floor. His heart started to pound. Someone was in his apartment. Slater climbed out of bed and went to the bedroom door, pulling it open and stepping out. It was the guy who'd come over last night, dressed now in his baggy jeans and that leather jacket, lying on his belly on the floor. His feet were together, his arms fully extended at his sides, his shaggy hair a mop on the grubby carpet. It was like looking at the wrong side of a biker version of the *Vitruvian Man.*

Slater put his hands on his hips. "What's going on?"

The guy sat up quickly and rubbed his eyes, as if he'd been asleep. "I was just praying." He pushed his hair back and looked Slater over. "Dude— you're all naked. Do you want to go again?"

"I've got stuff to do. You have to go."

The guy stood up. "Can I get your number?"

"Look for me on the app," Slater said, and gestured toward the door.

Once he'd hustled the guy out and flipped the deadbolt, he went to wash up, then stepped into the kitchen and opened the Frigidaire. The jar of instant coffee had only a few stray brown crumbs in the bottom, so he dropped it in the trash. A couple of little tubs of take-out salsa sat on the shelf, and he popped open the lid of one to smell the contents. Edible, he decided, and downed it, then fished a pickle out of the jar and crunched on it as he went to get dressed.

The jeans that lay rumpled on the bedroom floor were good for another day or so, and once he'd pulled them on, he squatted to tie his boots, then went to his closet to flip through his clean shirts. Rosa, the woman who came in to clean for him once in a while, had taken pity on him a while back and started to do his laundry. It was a canny move on her part, as he gladly paid her more to be free of the task.

A dark collared shirt, he decided, for a business meeting. Once he'd buttoned it, he locked his front door and trotted down the two flights to his garage. It was the main reason he stayed in this grungy little apartment—having a private space for his wheels and his gear was a rarity in gritty crowded Westlake.

Slater climbed into his classic black Thunderbird and backed into the alley, waiting for the heavy steel door to roll down before he drove toward the street. In a few blocks he crossed over the chasm of the 110 freeway, and once he was through downtown, pulled into the surface lot across the street from the building that housed his office.

As he climbed out, the parking lot attendant hustled toward him. Usually they left him alone because they recognized his car, and knew that he bought a monthly pass. Slater hadn't seen this guy before, squat and thick, with a pencil mustache, wearing a broad-brimmed straw hat.

As he stepped up, the guy said something in Spanish. It happened a lot—Slater had his father's dark Latin coloring, and thick black hair, and Spanish was the lingua franca in lots of this town. The only word he caught was *vaquero*.

"*No comprendo,* son," Slater said.

The guy frowned. "I'm older than you are, you condescending ass."

Slater had to grin. "What do you need?"

"It's fourteen for the day."

"I get a monthly pass." He sat in the driver's seat again to dig in the glovebox, and handed the guy the card.

"You should leave it in your windshield," he said, handing it back.

"And you should remember what my car looks like," Slater said, and climbed out again. "That way I won't have to punch you in the face."

The guy stood up straighter, watching warily as Slater dug in his pants pocket and palmed a twenty, then passed it to him. He hesitated for a moment, but then claimed it in a handshake, slapping Slater's hand.

"Thanks, boss," he said, his brow furrowing as he pocketed the bill. "I'll definitely remember you."

Slater hustled across the street when there was a break in the traffic, and stepped through the small crowd of day laborers in the lobby, waiting for sewing and cutting and carting jobs in the garment factories that filled the building. Up on the ninth floor, his office was the only one that wasn't about the clothing industry. He admired the lettering on the front door as he twisted his key in the lock.

SLATER IBÁÑEZ
MAXIMILLIAN CONROY
INVESTIGATIONS

Inside were three small offices—one for him, one for his business partner, Max, and the empty front office, with a desk that no one ever used. The only decoration out front was a small plaster statue of Rey Pascual, a skeleton holding a scythe and wearing a crown. It had been a gift from the woman he bought *pupusas* from, and Max obviously hadn't tired of it yet, as it was still sitting here, greeting anyone who came in the front door.

His partner wasn't in, he saw, briefly poking his head into Max's office before he went into his own. They collaborated sometimes, but mostly they worked separately, sharing resources like the office space, and spelling each other on lengthy boring stakeouts.

Sitting behind his desk, Slater pulled up the website for the *Sasquatch Search* podcast and read through the summaries of some of the team's expeditions. He clicked on a link for an episode preview, and Ryan's calm voice boomed from his computer's speakers, turned up too loud: *"These woods are dark and deep, but only a neophyte would call them lovely."*

As Slater hit the pause button so he could turn down the volume, Max stepped into his doorway. A burly guy, he was wearing his gray suit today with a yellow necktie. Since he'd found a girlfriend, his mousy brown hair was kept in a trendy cut. But with his gut hanging over his belt and the telltale bulge of a sidearm under his jacket, there was no mistaking his vocation—Max was a PI.

"I didn't hear you come in," Slater said, and sat back.

Max had a wry grin on his face. "Robert Frost? Have you gone all literary on me now?"

"Who's Robert Frost?"

"The poet. That audio clip is a riff on one of his works."

"You read poetry in your downtime?"

Max frowned and waved a hand. "It's pretty famous. One of those things everyone has to read in middle school."

"The clip is from a podcast I listen to sometimes. The narrator is coming in this morning to discuss a case. I'm boning up on his work."

"*Ka-ching,*" Max said. "What kind of podcast?"

"It's called *Sasquatch Search.*"

"Oh, you have to tell me about this one," he said, and pulled out the chair in front of Slater's desk, and sat down. "What's his ask?"

"I don't know yet. The narrator is a guy named

Ryan. He's kind of the team leader, although the decision-making process is quasi-democratic. Ryan decides whether the leads they get are legit, and he handles logistics, like booking flights and cars. Usually high-clearance four-wheel-drives to get into the backwoods. He likes Land Rovers."

"It sounds like they have a budget," Max said. "They're not just bored teenagers."

"And that means he should be able to pay me."

Max nodded. "Who else is on the team?"

"There's Marvel-Anne. She runs the technology: night-vision scopes, radios, paranormal frequency detectors."

"Of course you'd need a few of those. Do they have Sasquatches south of the Mason-Dixon Line? From her name, she sounds like a Southerner."

"They did an investigation in the Ozarks once, and the Okefenokee Swamp, but it's mostly in the Northwest. And Marvel-Anne is from Fresno."

"I like her already." Max chuckled. "Who else?"

"The only other person on the team is Kawamura. He handles security. He used to work at a casino in Vegas."

"So he's legit security."

"He doesn't talk much, and they never say anything about a weapon, but I'm certain that guy is strapped."

"Have they ever found any Sasquatches?"

"Not yet," Slater said. "I think the point of the podcast is more about the quest than the results. They hear Sasquatch sometimes, howling in the next valley, or over the ridge. They've found evidence in the woods. Hair and broken tree branches."

Max nodded. "Broken branches are extremely paranormal."

"I don't judge. I listen because it's so different from life here, hearing about them tramping around in the woods."

A sharp knock sounded at the front door, and Slater got up and went to answer it. Ryan was younger than he expected, in his mid-thirties, and lanky, with a bit of stubble and shaggy dirty-blond hair. Basically fuckable, Slater decided, looking him over.

"Slater?" he said, his brow furrowed with concern.

"Come on in."

"I thought I had the wrong place," he said, stepping inside. Towering behind his head was a blue canvas bag—he was wearing a big backpack, the kind people carried on lengthy camping trips. "I almost didn't come upstairs. The whole neighborhood is clothing stores, and your building is all sweatshops."

"'Sweatshops' implies forced labor and low pay," Max said, from the doorway of his office.

"Most of these businesses pay union wages."

"I stand corrected," Ryan said, eyeing him.

"This is Max, my business partner," Slater said.

They exchanged greetings, and Max went in to his desk. Slater led Ryan into his own office, pushing the door closed so that Max wouldn't have to listen to them. Ryan slung off his bag and propped it against the wall, then sat down and took a deep breath.

"Long trip?" Slater said, dropping into his chair.

"Not really. I came from Eugene. But your airport is overwhelming."

"The general consensus is that it's a civic embarrassment. Have you eaten?"

"I'm fine, but maybe a coffee?"

"We don't have a sink, but I can send out for it."

"Don't bother," Ryan said, and shot him a tired smile. He closed his eyes for a second, and muttered under his breath, "Focus."

Slater waited while the guy steadied himself. The process was interesting to watch. Some people just couldn't shift gears very quickly. When Ryan opened his eyes, they were visibly darker.

"You said you were looking for a missing person," Slater said.

Ryan nodded. "One of my team. Marvel-Anne. I know she's in LA."

"Did you talk to the police?"

"It's not that kind of missing. She's AWOL from our work. Her phone is still on, but she won't take my calls."

"Are you romantically involved?"

"We're close, but it's platonic." Ryan sat forward, holding his gaze. "We've worked together for years. It's extremely unusual that she just disappeared with no explanation. It means something hinky happened. I need to talk to her."

"Have you talked to her family?"

He sat back. "I wish I could. I don't really know any of them."

"Did you have an argument with her, or a disagreement?"

"Nothing like that. We wrapped up an expedition on the Washougal River. It's in Washington State. Afterward, we checked into a bed-and-breakfast in a little town, and spent a couple days there editing the audio. The plan was that we were going to check out of the place in the morning, to head back to civilization, and *poof,* she was gone. No explanation."

"Did anyone see her leave?" Slater said.

"The B&B host said she left at dawn, alone, with her backpack. Everyone was still sleeping. The woman asked her if she was checking out, and Marvel-Anne told her that I would take care of it when I woke up."

"Did she have her own wheels?"

"We drove up there in the same vehicle," Ryan said, his brow furrowing. "The host didn't see where she went, or whether she took a cab, or had a ride."

"What about Kawamura?"

Ryan shook his head. "He wasn't with us. The day we came out of the woods, he drove back to Portland. He doesn't hang around for sound editing."

"Is that process always a collaborative task with you and Marvel-Anne?"

"That's right."

"Don't you go on hiatus for the winter? It starts to snow up there in October, doesn't it? Maybe she decided it was time for that."

"The work doesn't stop for the weather. We usually move south at this time of year. Georgia and the Carolinas. I've got a lead in the Smoky Mountains that I want to pursue. It's getting stale with every passing hour."

The guy was more human, more fallible than his calm and deliberate podcast persona, Slater thought, watching him speak.

"Where's home for Marvel-Anne?"

"Portland. At least it was." He shook his head. "I went to see her roommate. She said Marvel-Anne took all her stuff and moved out. No forwarding address. That happened the same day she left the bed-and-breakfast."

"How do you know Marvel-Anne is in Los Angeles?" Slater said.

"She took an audio recorder with her. It has a GPS tracker built in to it. The location showed that she was here in LA for several days, and then it went offline."

"Why does your tech have a GPS tracker?"

"It's a security measure. We have quite a bit of high-end audio gear, and it's extremely portable, and extremely expensive. That unit alone is worth three grand."

"Does Marvel-Anne know it has a GPS tracker?"

"We never had to use it, so maybe not. I know we never discussed that specifically. She handled the audio equipment, but I'm the one who bought it, and made sure I could track it."

"What about Kawamura?" Slater said. "What does he know?"

"About Marvel-Anne, nothing. I called him right after she disappeared."

"Where is he now?"

"I think he's with his parents in Seattle. I don't actually know him that well."

"How is that possible? He's with you on every expedition."

"That's not completely true," Ryan said, his cheeks visibly reddening. "We edit the episodes so that it's not obvious that he's not around. Sometimes he'll walk us in to a camp and assess the safety, and then leave before we do, on his own. But he always stays with us when we're in the deep woods, way off the beaten path."

"I guess that's why he doesn't talk that much."

"He's also a taciturn person. It's not ideal for an audio medium like podcasting, right, but he's good at keeping us calm, and he's competent at what he does."

"Does he carry a weapon?" Slater said.

"Always. In a shoulder holster." Ryan extended a finger and poked it under his arm. "I don't know guns, or what kind it is, but it's modern."

"What do you mean by that?"

"It's not one of those Wild West six-shooters. It's more like what you see the police carry. Square lines rather than a revolver."

Slater shifted in his chair. "So what I'm hearing is, Marvel-Anne ditched you and moved out of her place to do her own thing, but she's not actually in any danger, because she left of her own volition. She's an adult—if she doesn't want to talk to you, why pursue her?"

"Because what she's done is completely out of character. Something weird happened. I know she's probably all right, or I would have heard. But I need her to tell me why she left."

"You can't make her come back to work. I'm

not sure I can help you."

Ryan sat forward and held his gaze. "All I need is to talk to her. Even for a minute. I need an explanation. If she's done with our work, I can accept that. But I need to hear it."

"Bad news is better than no news at all," Slater offered.

"Exactly."

"Do you have any money?"

"That's not an issue," Ryan said. "I can pay you."

"I always wondered how you could afford to pursue the quest full-time. There's not that much advertising on the podcast. Are you a trust-fund baby?"

"Did you listen to the podcast in the early days, before I brought Marvel-Anne and Kawamura on board?"

"I don't think so."

"I've always been all about bigfoot, ever since I was twelve years old, when I read about it in a book. When I started the podcast, I mostly had secondhand information. I talked about potential sites to look for the creature—tips I got about places where campers or rangers or biologists had spotted evidence. I went to a few of the locations, and I always came up short because I had to get back to my desk job. I mentioned on the podcast how frustrating that was, that limitation. One day a lawyer contacted me and told me she had an anonymous donor who wanted to fund the work."

"Sweet. How much did they pay you?"

"A hundred grand," Ryan said. "Two years later it got renewed. I have to run it as a non-profit, and check in with the lawyer once in a while to show her where the money's going, but the return on the investment for the donor is in the podcast episodes."

"This person doesn't have editorial input?"

"Zero."

"And you have no idea who it is?"

Ryan shook his head.

"That's a great story."

"So what are you going to cost me?"

"I haven't said I'll help you yet."

"Will you help me?" Ryan said intently.

Those eyes were so earnest. It was hard to say no to such a pretty face. That shouldn't influence a rational decision, Slater knew that, but this guy seemed pretty messed up over the situation.

"I'll see what I can do," he said finally.

Ryan slumped back and cracked a smile. "That's very good news."

"If I'm at it full-time, it'll cost you five hundred a day. Give me two grand to start. I work in cash."

"I don't walk around with that kind of money,"

Ryan said, and frowned. "Can't I just zap it to your bank account?"

"If you must." Slater pulled open his desk drawer and found a business card, then slid it across the desk. "My phone number should work."

Ryan pulled out his phone and tapped at it, briefly glancing at the card. A moment later Slater's phone buzzed in his pants. It was a notification about the incoming transfer, he saw, when he pulled it out to check.

"Got it," Slater said, and set his phone down. "You said you have the GPS tracker data for the audio equipment."

"It's on my computer. Do you want me to pull it up?"

"Eventually. First, is there anything else you know about Marvel-Anne's connections in LA? Does she have family or friends here?"

"I know of one contact," Ryan said. "A sorority sister who lives here. She works with furniture. Marvel-Anne reached out to her when we were trying to figure out why Sasquatch manipulated larch trees differently than ponderosa pines. We asked her about the properties of the wood."

"Where did they go to school?"

"Cal State Fresno. That's where Marvel-Anne was in the sorority. After that, she went to graduate school at Caltech."

Slater raised his eyebrows. "Marvel-Anne went to Caltech?"

"You look surprised. Is it because she's black? That's a private school, but it's not segregated anymore. It sounds like you're working under some racist assumptions."

"Listen," Slater said intently, leaning on the desk. "One, I didn't know Marvel-Anne was black, and two, I'm not going to be taking instructions on getting woke from an entitled cisgender white guy."

Ryan frowned. "Dude—chill. I'm sure she's talked about race and ethnicity on the podcast."

"I tune in, but it's late at night. I don't absorb all the details. I mostly listen because of you, and your voice."

"Aw." He grinned, and then pulled out his phone and swiped at it, and handed it to Slater. "Here's a photo of her."

Slater studied the image. Ryan and a tall buff guy flanked a curvy woman with dark-rimmed glasses, her hair tied above her head in a bundle. That was Marvel-Anne, and the big guy had to be Kawamura. He was a few years older than the other two. Marvel-Anne was tall as well, he realized, as she stood the same height as Ryan. All three of them were smiling at the camera, their arms around each other. Conifers formed the backdrop, and they were dressed for camping, in plaid and denim. It's how Slater pictured them from the podcast—on an expedition, out in the woods somewhere.

"Send me a copy of that," Slater said. "What do we know about this sorority sister?"

"Her name is Im Hae," he said, and spelled it.

Slater shook his head. "Koreans are tough to track down. There's half a million of them in this town, and most have the same five family names."

"I know what her business is called."

"That makes it easier." Slater turned to his computer and added, "Hit me."

"It's a place called Neglected Treasures. I'm not sure if it's wholesale or retail."

Slater typed and stared at the screen. "There's a furniture dealer with that name, and it has a street address in Koreatown."

"That has to be her. It all fits. Where's Koreatown?"

"Not far from here."

"Let's go."

"Don't you need to sleep," Slater said, eyeing him, "or take some downtime?"

"I don't really do time off. Can't I come with you?"

"I work alone. The people who hire me don't usually want to see how I do what I do."

"I'm sure I can handle it," Ryan said. "We're just going to talk to her, right?"

Slater locked his computer with a keystroke and stood up. "Fine—but I'm going to talk to her. You're going to keep your mouth shut."

As Slater stepped out, and stood in Max's doorway, Ryan rose to follow him. Max looked up from his computer screen.

"Can you ask Vanessa if she knows the woman we're trying to track down?" Slater said. "She went to grad school at Caltech." To Ryan, he said, "Max's girlfriend is a professor there."

"Your girlfriend is a prof at Caltech?" Ryan said, eyeing him.

"Adjunct," Max said, his eyes narrowing.

"Now who's operating on biased assumptions?" Slater demanded. He took a framed photo from Max's desk and handed it to him.

Ryan peered at the image of Max and Vanessa for a moment before he handed it back.

"You're a lucky man," Ryan said. "She's beautiful."

"I know," Max said, and frowned. "I'll need a name."

"Marvel-Anne Willits."

THREE

ᘰᘰᘰᘰᘰᘰᘰᘰᘰᘰ

ONCE THEY WERE ACROSS the street, Slater got in behind the wheel of his car and reached over to unlock the passenger door for Ryan.

"Sweet ride," he said, climbing in. "How old is it?"

"It's a '78."

"T-birds had a big engine, as I remember."

"It definitely knows how to accelerate."

"Does it have a name?"

"Like a kid, or a pet?" Slater said, nosing into the street. "I never did that with my wheels."

"People who name their cars tend to take better care of them."

"With a classic car it's all about managing wear and tear. I've got a guy for that."

Slater drove west, to Koreatown, turning onto Western Avenue and cruising along in the right lane. This stretch of the boulevard was a dense warren of shops, with driveways between the buildings that led to more shops.

"It should be right around here," he said, pulling into a curb space. As they both got out, he met Ryan's gaze. "Remember—I do the talking."

"Exclusively? I'm not sure that's wise. You don't know Marvel-Anne."

"Do not second-guess me, toots," Slater said intently. "I know what I'm doing."

Walking up the driveway, he scanned the numbers on the doorways. As they got deeper into the block, the spaces became commercial entities without the retail markings, many of them named only in Korean script. Finally he found the right number, stenciled in black on a solid steel door. There was nothing to indicate the name of the business, but when he twisted the handle, it was unlocked, and he stepped inside.

The big room had a high ceiling with skylights that lit rows of old furniture—an array of desks and dressers and tables. Some of it was mid-century, and some art deco, but none of it was junk, Slater saw, although only a few of the pieces had been refinished. Most of it looked like it needed restoration work.

The only person in sight was near the back, wearing jeans and a gray hoodie, standing over a low dresser with a belt sander in her gloved hands. As they stepped inside, she set down the tool and pulled her respirator onto her forehead.

"Can I help you?"

Slater stepped toward her. "You're Im Hae?"

"That's me."

"What's with Guanyin?" he said, gesturing to a small plaster statue of the goddess, standing upright on a table next to a crazed floor mirror. "I thought Koreans were mostly into Christ."

"It's not that black-and-white," she said. "Everybody there has a little Daoism and a little Buddhism in them. And her Korean name is Guan-eum. How do you know her?"

"I worked a job where she got involved."

"Make me an offer, if you want it. For me it's just a piece of art to sell. Although I actually am Buddhist."

"Not the statue-worshipping kind?" Ryan said.

Im Hae gestured vaguely. "It's hard to explain. Buddhism is mysterious and mystical."

"Bullshit," Slater said. "Something is only mystical if you don't know anything about it. Like churches, and unicycles, and tampons. I know what they're for, but I have no firsthand experience. That doesn't make them mystical."

She laughed. "I like that. I'm going to use it

in a poem. 'Mystical mysterious tampon.' Who are you two?"

"I'm a friend of Marvel-Anne Willits," Ryan said. "Have you talked to her lately?"

Slater shot him a murderous glare.

"Who's asking?" Im Hae jutted her chin.

"My name is Ryan."

"You do the podcast with her."

"That's right. Marvel-Anne interviewed you about larch wood."

"I remember," she said, and shrugged. "I don't really listen to the show."

"Marvel-Anne came to LA, and she's not answering my calls. I'm worried about her."

She raised her eyebrows. "Did you ever consider that she might not want to talk to you?"

"That makes no sense," Ryan said. "She never said anything like that."

"I can't help you, brother. Even if I could, I wouldn't."

Slater threw up his hands. "See, this is why I work alone." He stepped toward the workbench that ran along the wall and picked up a heavy maul, feeling its heft with both hands. "Why do you have a post maul?"

"It's called a sledgehammer," Im Hae said, eyeing him warily.

"It's a post maul," Slater said firmly. "Do you use this on furniture?"

"Put it down, cowboy."

Slater heaved the maul onto his shoulder and looked around the room. "You seem like a sensible person, Im Hae. I really need more from you. I'd hate to mess this place up."

"Are you kidding me?" she said. "If you try anything like that, I'm calling the cops."

"The problem is, it'll take them a while to get here, and by then I'll be through a good chunk of your inventory, and out the door, and in the wind." He slid his hand up the shaft, near the head, and lifted the maul off his shoulder. "But it's up to you. I'm thinking it would be easier for everyone if you just told me what you know."

Im Hae folded her arms and scowled at him—a tacit challenge. Slater heaved the maul high over his head, grasping the end of the handle with two fingers, and let the head free-fall onto one end of a nearby sawhorse. It struck with a reverberating *crack*, and the legs at that end snapped apart, and the structure collapsed.

"You fucking psycho," Im Hae shouted. "Do you know what those things cost?"

Ryan stood staring at him, wide-eyed. "Slater," he said. "Come on."

Slater shot him a furious look. That was a stupid thing to do—now she knew his name.

"What's next?" Slater said. "Is that cabinet Danish?"

Im Hae held her palms out at her sides. "I haven't seen Marvel-Anne," she said quickly. "I haven't heard from her in ages."

"Who does she know in LA?" Slater demanded.

"The only person I met was one of her friends who works at a bookstore in La Mirada. We drove down there once. I don't remember the friend's name, but the shop is called Armada Books."

"How is it that you remember that," Slater said, "but not the person's name?"

Im Hae waved an arm. "It was a whole thing."

"Sing, sister," Slater said, and swung the maul up onto his shoulder.

"Relax," she snapped. "The story was that the new owner of the store wanted it to have a new name. Changing it from La Mirada Books to Armada Books meant she didn't have to buy any new letters for the sign—she could just rearrange them."

"Is this friend a man or a woman?" Ryan said.

"A whole lot of woman," Im Hae said, eyeing him and raising her eyebrows. "Tall, and Latin, with luxurious dark hair. Short skirt and gams for days."

"And yet you don't remember her name," Slater said.

"I wasn't looking at her name."

Slater set down the maul. "How hard was

that?" he demanded, and strode toward the door.

Ryan hurried to follow him out to the street. Once they'd climbed into the Thunderbird, Slater started the engine.

"I told you to hold your tongue," he said sharply, glancing over at him as he pulled into the traffic.

"All I told her was why we were there."

"That's not how I do things."

"I didn't know you were going to start smashing stuff," Ryan said. "That was intense."

"I warned you about that."

"I was afraid of what you were going to do next."

"Her response to doing it your way was nada," Slater said. "A stone wall. My way worked."

"I thought we were both going to get arrested."

"I wouldn't have let that happen." He eyed Ryan sidelong as he braked for a red light. "Focus on the fact that I got results. That's why you hired me."

Ryan made a helpless gesture. "It is. You're right."

"From now on, you do what I say."

"Fine." He sighed. "Are you hungry at all?"

"Do you like *bibimbap*?" Slater said. "There's a decent place near here."

"I don't know what that is."

"Rice and veggies in a hot stone bowl. You'll

love it."

As Slater drove, Ryan pulled out his phone and tapped at it.

"I found the bookstore," he said. "How far is Mirada?"

"It's La Mirada. About an hour."

"So it's far."

"It's actually really close," Slater said. "But there's always traffic."

"The place is closing soon anyway. I guess people there don't need books after dinner."

"We can hit it tomorrow."

Ryan looked over at him. "Right on."

Slater found a spot to park in the restaurant's tiny lot, and they climbed out.

"It looks like a pancake house," Ryan said.

"Los Angeles has always been about reinvention. It might have been a pancake place in a former life, but now it's all about *bibimbap*."

Near the doorway, a guy in work clothes was planting seedlings in the raised wooden boxes under the windows. It was an odd time of day to be doing that, with the long shadows of evening stretching across the parking lot.

"Is that black sage?" Slater said, pausing to look at the box.

"It's Mexican sage," he said, straightening up and wiping the back of his gloved hand across his brow.

"Good choice. It's showy."

"It will be by spring, at least."

"If you interplant black sage," Slater said, "you'll get the scent along with the color. *Bam*, two for one."

His brow furrowed. "I like that idea. It might actually work."

Once they were inside, and sitting in the booth that the host had pointed out, Ryan said, "You're a gardener too?"

"I trained in horticulture, and worked in it for a while. But dealing with lowlifes pays better."

"Is everybody who makes an insurance claim a lowlife?"

"I only get called in on sticky cases. When the pencil-pushers smell fraud. On those ones, they're always lowlifes."

The waitress stepped over, and Slater told her, "Two veggie bowls, one without egg."

Once she'd left, Ryan said, "You don't like eggs?"

"I'm vegan."

"Really? There are lots of those people in Portland. You don't look like a vegan."

"You don't look like the kind of person I'd punch in the face, and yet it just might happen."

Ryan frowned. "What's with the violence? We're just talking. I half believed you were going to smash up Im Hae's furniture back there."

Slater paused as another waiter set down a trio of little side dishes in metal bowls.

"She would have started talking once I'd gone through a piece or two," he said. "I had my eye on that tall dresser. It looked flimsy. It would have made a good show—splinters everywhere."

Ryan snapped apart his chopsticks and dug into the little bowl of pickles. "I had a disagreement with this Buddhist guy once. He told me, 'You need to go nourish yourself.' It was the harshest thing he could come up with." He gestured to the bowls. "So nourish yourself. Eat some snacks."

Slater chuckled and grabbed his chopsticks. It was interesting that Ryan wasn't easily intimidated. Sometimes that meant a person had seen a lot of action, and knew how to handle it. But this guy didn't have that edge. He was a civilian— his blithe confidence meant he'd grown up with privilege, in a safe warm bubble, and never had to scrap for scarce resources.

When the main dish arrived, in steaming-hot iron bowls, Ryan said, "How do I eat it?"

"Just stir it up and dig in."

"I wonder sometimes if that's part of Sasquatch culture," Ryan said, once he'd taken a few mouthfuls. "Maybe Sasquatch destroys things for the cathartic release. Like you smashing that sawhorse."

"If you've never actually found the Sasquatch,

how do you know they destroy things? Or have culture?"

"I've seen plenty of evidence." He raised his eyebrows. "Six-inch-thick Douglas fir trees twisted into toothpicks. And they make art, which means they have culture. Decorative assemblages of twigs."

"Why is bigfoot so hard to find?"

"As the years go by, and I learn more, I'm starting to think it might be a paranormal entity."

Slater eyed him. He was being serious. "Meaning what?"

"I'm not sure." Ryan stirred the food in his bowl. "An example is that they might be able to disappear at will."

"You mean they turn invisible?"

"Or they phase out of existence, or they time-travel, or they teleport. Or all of the above. I'm not sure. But Sasquatch is no ordinary creature."

"You interviewed a guy once on the podcast who believed that."

"Big Jim," Ryan said. "He developed a lot of the theories about bigfoot's liminal nature."

"He also said Sasquatches ride around in flying saucers, and follow him in his car, hovering behind him in their invisible ships. No one could see them, but he knew they were there."

Ryan gestured with his chopsticks. "Not all of it is immediately intuitive."

"Or plausible."

He laughed. "Fair enough."

"I'm not saying I dismiss your ideas," Slater said. "I can't do that—you know more about the phenomenon than anyone. You've spent so much time on it."

"That's a great outlook. There's more to it as well. I'm playing a small part in a much larger cultural shift."

"Bigfoot's big reveal?" Slater said, setting his chopsticks aside.

"Bigger than that. A sea change in the human psyche, where we're becoming aware of intangible things, and accepting that reality isn't just what we see."

"That sounds kind of New Age."

"That stuff is about belief," Ryan said, waving a hand. "I'm talking about quantifiable reality. It happened before at several points. Sometimes it sparks a religious revival, like the New Age, but religion is a reaction to these shifts, not the cause. They happen at a deeper level."

"When did it happen before?"

"Well, a big one was around 1877. The telephone and the phonograph were invented at almost the same moment. Suddenly you could hear someone's voice separated from them in space, and you could record a voice to hear later, separated from the person in time." He leaned forward. "Imagine life before that—you'd only ever hear a person's voice face-to-face, never from a distance, and never from the past. Now, suddenly, your voice could be separated from your body both in time and in space. It caused a major shift in human consciousness."

"I guess that would have been mind-blowing," Slater said, watching him eat.

Eventually Ryan set his chopsticks down.

"You look tired," Slater said.

"I am tired. It's dark out already."

"So we'll go to my office to get your bag, and pick up again tomorrow."

Walking out to the car, Slater's phone buzzed in his pants. It was a text from Max:

Vanessa doesn't know your target. She might have graduated before Vanessa got there.

On the drive through downtown, Ryan gazed out the window, watching the lights of the city roll by.

"Do you know where the Balfour Hotel is?"

"Not far," Slater said. "Are you staying there?"

"Not yet, but I found it online. It's big, right, so I'm sure they'll have a room for me."

"You don't want to stay there. It's overpriced, and it's due for a renovation."

"I'm used to roughing it. I camp in the woods about a hundred nights a year."

Slater pulled up to the curb in front of his building, quiet at this hour, and eyed Ryan as he killed the engine.

"They found a body in the water supply tank on the roof a while back. The guests were complaining about the funky taste."

"Gross."

"If you're used to rough places," Slater said, "you can crash on my sofa. It's not pretty, but it's free, and it's better than the Balfour."

"That sounds great. Thanks, man."

The lobby of his building was empty, and as they waited for the elevator, Ryan pointed at the notice board on the wall, checkered with an array of sticky notes.

"What are those?"

"Jobs for the day laborers for tomorrow."

"Your partner said these were union workers."

"I guess not all of them."

"This building wasn't always for the clothing business, I bet," Ryan said, stepping onto the elevator. "It would have been a white-collar office building in the art deco era."

"That's exactly how old it is. When we found this place, there were still bolts set in the concrete floor in my office to install a safe."

"That's definitely old-school. It's fitting that you and Max are here. Your business is as old as civilization itself."

Slater looked him over, saw his eyes hooded with exhaustion, his solid pecs. The guy was intelligent, and self-confident, and hot. But he couldn't get interested in a client, not in that way. He was already getting too close, inviting him to stay at his place.

Once he'd unlocked the office door, Slater stepped inside and flipped on the lights.

"What does the statue mean?" Ryan said, pointing to it.

"His name is Rey Pascual. He's from Latin America."

"He's a Catholic saint?"

"I think he was here long before the Catholics were."

Slater stepped briefly into Max's office, then went to his own.

"Why is he wearing a crown?" Ryan called to him.

"Because he's the king of the graveyard."

Slater lifted up the bulky backpack and handed it to Ryan.

"Why did you look into your partner's office?" he said, heaving the bag onto his back and pulling the thick straps onto his shoulders. "The lights were off when we came in."

"It's common sense. You never know what's going on. Lights or no lights, you need to stay aware of your surroundings."

"So suspicious," Ryan said. "Your job permeates everything."

Slater locked the door behind them. "So does yours. It's not just the quest for bigfoot. You've got lots of questions about everything else."

Ryan chuckled. "I guess that's true."

FOUR

ONCE HE'D PARKED IN his garage, Slater led the way up the stairs to his apartment. Ryan lagged behind, weighed down by his pack. As they stepped inside, Ryan looked the place over.

"Your sofa is long enough for me to stretch out. That's all I need. It's perfect."

"You might change your mind when you see the shower," Slater said, bolting the door. "It's a little grungy."

"I sleep out in the woods half the time. At least it's warm in here."

Slater put his hands on his hips. "I remember you talking about lying in your tent, and watching the stars through the mosquito netting on the rare nights when it wasn't raining."

"You actually do listen, huh," Ryan said, and smiled.

"I don't retain much, but I remember that image. Let me get you some sheets."

He stepped into the bedroom and pulled a sheet and a blanket and a pillow from the top shelf of the closet.

"There's a word in Yiddish," Ryan called to him. "*Schnorrer.* It means a freeloader. I feel like that—I'm freeloading."

"You're not schnorring off me," Slater said, stepping back into the room. "There's nothing to take, except tap water." He handed Ryan the bundle. "Are you Jewish?"

"Ish. My father was." He dropped the pillow and blanket on the recliner and opened the sheet over the sofa.

"I'm halfway there too. On my mother's side."

"Then you're more entitled to it than me. Were you bar-mitzvahed?"

Slater nodded. "Oh, yeah."

"There's no half measure about that."

"Do you want a drink? All I've got is bourbon. I'm going to have my nightly ration."

"Why do you ration it?"

"I've got booze rules." Slater ran a hand through his hair. "So that I don't overindulge. It's either that, or get brainwashed at some organic-sisal rehab place, or sit around in a circle with a bunch of junkies talking about their feelings."

Ryan tossed the pillow onto his makeshift bed. "It sounds like you've got it figured out. I'm wiped out—I just need to sleep."

"Suit yourself," Slater said, and went to the kitchen cupboard, and pulled out the fifth. Since he wasn't going to linger, he didn't bother to pour it into a glass, and drank from the bottle, resisting the urge to cough as the amber elixir burned in his nose and his throat.

Ryan had his shoes off and his shirt unbuttoned, Slater saw, and watched him for a moment as he squatted to untie the top of his big pack.

"Good night, narrator," he said finally, and went into his bedroom.

He hesitated at the door, then decided to close it. It was weird to have a guest who wasn't here for sex. He wasn't sure he'd be able to fall asleep with just the one belt of bourbon, but he got undressed anyway and killed the lights.

Sometime later he woke, adrenaline surging in his body. Something was wrong. He lay motionless, listening, trying to figure it out. In the dim light from the hazy window he saw a figure at his bedside, naked, holding his own biceps, and trembling. Ryan.

"Are you OK?" Slater mumbled.

"I'm cold."

"Do you need another blanket?"

"It's not about that."

Slater wanted to see the expression on his face, but it was too dark. He pulled back the covers and shifted over. Ryan climbed in beside him, tentatively touching his arm. His cold fingers made Slater start.

"I'm sorry," he said, under his breath.

The guy was practically vibrating, like he had a chill. Slater reached for his knee, and using a wrestling technique, deftly shifted him onto his side, eliciting a gasp of surprise. Wrapping an arm around his chest, he slid the other under his neck, and notched his knees into Ryan's, and held firm. It seemed to help, as the trembling gradually started to ebb.

This guy was more messed up than what he presented to the world, Slater realized. He could understand that, in a way. Nighttime was long, and silent, and wide open. It could be hard for anyone.

He woke again when Ryan rolled onto his back. His skin felt warm, and he wasn't shivering anymore.

"I sense a local uprising," Ryan said.

It was true—Slater had a raging woody, poking into Ryan's thigh.

"An involuntary reaction," Slater mumbled.

Ryan grabbed his cock, and squeezed, and hesitated a moment before he met Slater's mouth.

He was hard too, Slater realized, as Ryan ground into him. His tongue was hot, exploring Slater's mouth, and his jaw, and then his neck. Slater took hold of his cock and gently stroked it.

"Have you got a condom?" Ryan said, his voice breathy.

"In the drawer."

He rolled to the side of the futon and scrabbled for it in the dark, then turned back and tore it open, and rolled it onto Slater. A moment later he felt a handful of cold lube, and then Ryan straddled him, groaning as he sank down onto him, guiding Slater into him.

Slater grabbed his cock and stroked it as Ryan rocked back and forth on top of him.

"I'm doing this for you," Ryan said, his tone an accusation.

"I get it." Slater reached up and put his hand behind his neck. A minute later Ryan yelped and came, then grabbed Slater's hand to stop him. Watching him was hot, and Slater came too, straining up into him.

Collapsing on top of him, Ryan's hot breath rattled in Slater's ear, gradually slowing. Slater drifted off, but woke again when Ryan got up, and went to find a towel, and returned with it to clean them both up. When he was done he threw the cloth on the floor and stretched out next to Slater.

"Listen," he began, but Slater shifted, interrupting him.

Slater wrapped an arm around his chest and pulled him closer.

"It's late," he said. "You're safe. Everything's OK."

FIVE

AYLIGHT STREAMED IN THE window when Slater woke, back-to-back with a warm body. They didn't always stay overnight. He wondered idly who it was. Then the flood of memory rushed in, and he flipped onto his back.

Ryan turned toward him, and saw that he was awake. "So, that happened."

"It doesn't change anything," Slater said.

"Do we need to talk about it?"

"I don't. But you can, if you really have to."

Ryan took a breath and caressed his arm. "I guess I don't need to," he said finally. "You seem cavalier about it."

"I sleep around a lot."

"That might explain it." He gently ran his

fingers across Slater's belly. "I guess I've got problems."

Slater scoffed. "Hot people don't have problems."

Ryan met his gaze. "You think I'm hot?"

"Do not even pretend like you don't know you are. Pretty things are automatically insulated from strife, but there's no excuse for being unaware of that."

"You don't know my experiences. And hotness might be more subjective than you think."

"I thought we didn't need to talk about it."

Ryan sat up. "Can I make coffee?"

"I don't have any. There are lots of places out."

"I'll get dressed." Ryan rose and walked into the other room.

Watching his naked form as he left, Slater saw that he had a tattoo across his shoulders, vivid green ink in an undulating pattern. He'd have to take a closer look at that.

Once he'd washed up and pulled on his own clothes, Slater came out to find Ryan wearing chinos and a short-sleeved plaid shirt.

"It might be cold for that," Slater said. "It's winter."

Ryan grinned. "I checked the weather. It's going to be sixty-eight today."

"That's winter."

"In Oregon, it's short-sleeve weather."

"Suit yourself," Slater said. "Bring your computer."

"Got it," Ryan said, and lifted a slender green day pack onto his shoulder.

Down in the garage, they climbed into the Thunderbird, and Slater headed out to the boulevard.

"It's so bright here," Ryan said. "I bet people don't need so much caffeine. In Oregon and Washington there's coffee everywhere. Every little town. Even on the highway in the woods, they're selling it out of a trailer."

"There's java near my office," Slater said.

Once he'd pulled into the lot across from his building, Slater climbed out and waved to the attendant, over in the little booth. It was the guy who'd challenged him yesterday, watching him from under his straw hat, and he nodded in reply.

The coffee place was in the next block. On the way inside, Ryan said, "What are you having?"

"Get me a soy latte."

As he stepped up to the counter, Ryan greeted the clerk. "How are you this fine morning?"

"I'm OK," she said, frowning suspiciously. "What can I get you?"

Unfazed, Ryan ordered, and thanked her in the same chipper tone. Slater had to grin. He was a small-town guy, friendly to everyone. The clerk likely assumed he was high on something.

Ryan picked up their cups and joined Slater near the door. "Do you want to sit here?"

"We'll go to my office."

They walked back to his building and through the phalanx of day laborers waiting for work. Upstairs, the lights were off, and after he glanced into Max's empty space, Slater went into his own.

As Ryan stepped in behind him, he glanced at the statue on the desk in the front office and said, "Morning, Rey."

"It's an inanimate object," Slater said, as he sat behind his desk. "He can't hear you."

He shrugged. "You never know."

"Show me the GPS data from the audio gear that Marvel-Anne had."

Ryan slipped his bag off as he sat down, and pulled his laptop out of it. He set the device on the edge of Slater's desk, and once he had it running, clicked and peered at the screen, eventually twisting it around for Slater to see. It was the interface for a security product, showing a lengthy list of dates and latitude-longitude coordinates.

"This is where the LA data starts," he said, and pointed to a row halfway down. "There are a bunch of hits, but it was all in the same place."

"Did it register during the trip down here?"

"It must have been under something, or inside a case, and not able to get a signal. The data shows that the unit was in Oregon, and then there's a gap of a couple of days, and then the data points in LA."

"So someone took it out of the case once it got here," Slater said. "What's the date range for LA?"

"Tuesday to Thursday last week."

"And no location data since then? Did someone put it away again?"

"I don't think so—the last entry is a low-battery warning," Ryan said. "The GPS unit feeds off the main battery. If you put it on a shelf, it gradually drains it. Seeing that warning and then no more GPS data probably means that nobody has plugged it into the charger."

On his own computer Slater pulled up a mapping site and typed in the coordinates.

"It's in West Hollywood," he said. "Inside a structure … it looks like an apartment building."

"Maybe Marvel-Anne is staying there. Should we go check it out, or should we go to the bookstore in La Mirada?"

Slater watched him for a moment. The bookstore was a weak lead, without an actual name, and only a vague description of Marvel-Anne's dark-haired friend. Im Hae easily could have invented her. But sending Ryan there would keep him from interfering with the better lead.

"Both," he said finally. "We should split up."

Ryan frowned. "Why?"

"Yesterday you gave that woman my name—right after I'd smashed her sawhorse."

"I don't remember that."

"Well, you did," Slater said. "It's the reason I work alone. I'll hit the address with the audio equipment, and you go check out the bookstore."

"All right." Ryan looked away. "At least I'll have the memory of you inside me."

"You liked that, huh." Slater watched him. Even though Ryan was the one who'd initiated sex, and the one who'd just brought it up, he was blushing. "Well, there's more where that came from."

"So can I get to La Mirada on public transportation?"

"Probably, but it'll take you half the day."

"So I should rent a car. That's easy enough. Is there a vendor in this neighborhood?"

"My vehicle is in the shop a lot, and my mechanic rents out cars. He's got more of them than he has room for. His place is near here. Do you have some cash?"

"A few hundred bucks."

"Let me call him." Slater pulled out his phone and dialed, glad that Duarte picked up. "I have a client who needs a vehicle for a couple days," he said.

"How about the '63 Polara?" Duarte said. "It's running great, and it needs some exercise."

Slater eyed Ryan. "Can you drive a stick?"

"Sure."

"The Polara will be fine. Can you bring it to my office?"

"Give me a few minutes," Duarte said. "Tell him cash only."

"What's a Polara?" Ryan said, when Slater set down his phone.

"It's a classic Dodge. You'll love it."

"Classic, like your car?"

"Much older. It's a '63."

Ryan waved his arm. "I can't drive an antique."

"It's easier to handle than those behemoths you rent on the podcast. It has that 361 V-8 engine."

"I don't know what that means."

"It's got plenty of pep." Slater sat forward. "Tell me what the audio equipment looks like. The machine that generated these GPS records."

"Marvel-Anne had a couple of devices," Ryan said, and sat up to look at his laptop.

A moment later he turned the screen so Slater could see the images. All of the components were small black boxes with intricate controls and inputs—professional gear rather than consumer stuff.

"Forward those to me," Slater said. On the desktop his phone buzzed, and he lifted it to check. "Duarte is downstairs. He brought your ride."

Ryan folded his computer closed and stuffed it in his backpack, then rose. "You know the guy—you have to come down with me."

In his top desk drawer Slater found the spare keys to his apartment, and pocketed them, then rose and walked with Ryan to the elevator.

On the ride down, Slater said, "Don't try to negotiate with him. Just pay what he asks."

"Why?"

"I have an existing business relationship with him."

"I guess that makes sense."

"There's no room for analysis here. Just do what I tell you."

When they stepped out to the street, two classic cars were parked at the curb—a tomato-red Polara in the loading zone, and in front of it, a powder-blue lowrider with tiny wheels and chrome rims.

"Please tell me it's the red one," Ryan said quietly.

Leaning against the Polara was Duarte, a skinny guy in board shorts and a bowling shirt, his long black hair bound behind his head. He greeted Slater, who introduced Ryan.

"It's beautiful," Ryan said, looking over the car, "but I'm not sure I should be driving a museum piece."

"You'll be fine," Slater said.

Duarte raised his eyebrows. "How long do you need it?"

"I'm thinking a couple of days."

"Give me one forty."

Without a word Ryan pulled out his wallet and extracted a C-note and some twenties, and Duarte handed him the car keys.

"I won't shake your hand," Duarte said, "because mine are covered with engine grease."

"Fist bump, then."

Duarte grinned and tapped his knuckles to Ryan's, spreading his fingers and making the sound of an explosion as he pulled his hand away.

"Insurance and registration are on the visor, and so is my number. Call me if you have any problems with it." To Slater, he added, "How's the T-bird?"

"Purring like a kitten."

"Good to hear." He nodded and glanced at the lowrider. "Later, *cabrón*."

They watched as he climbed in the passenger side, and the vehicle pulled away.

"*Cabrón* is a term of endearment?" Ryan said.

"I'm not really sure. My Spanish is pathetic."

"That guy likes you."

Slater scoffed. "Dude is straight. His wife was driving that Impala."

"I didn't mean it that way."

"Well, he should like me—I pay him plenty

to keep my car in shape." Digging in his pocket, he pulled out his spare keys and handed them to Ryan. "That's for the door to my apartment, and to get into the building."

"You're very hospitable."

He shrugged. "There's nothing to steal."

"I'm glad I can't be accused of that, then," Ryan said, and frowned.

"Do you have a navigation app on your phone?"

"I already looked up which highways to take to get to the bookstore."

"You still have to use an app. It'll route you around the traffic—and there's always traffic."

As Ryan stepped around the Polara to get behind the wheel, Slater went back inside. Upstairs at his desk, he took a breath. It felt good to be rid of that guy for a while.

The GPS data for the audio equipment indicated a precise point, and when Slater looked again at the satellite view of the location, he saw that it was definitely inside an apartment building. Zooming in, the marker was near the back corner, on the right side. If he went there, with any luck he'd be able to figure out which unit it was.

When he got down to the street, the Polara was gone, and he hustled across to the surface lot. Traffic was fluid on the 101 toward Hollywood, and it didn't take long to get to WeHo. Pulling up in front of the building, he saw that it was one of those postwar courtyard complexes. So many of these had been built fast, light, and cheap in that era. He climbed out of his car and found that the front gate was ajar, so he walked in.

Some of these buildings had a swimming pool in the middle, but this one was too small for that, and instead had a dribbling fountain surrounded by a lush garden, planted with a few palm trees and lots of thirsty nonnatives. He stopped to examine the growth in a raised bed. Some kind of *Vinca*. Probably periwinkle—people loved those. It didn't belong here, and it was such a waste of resources, as it only flowered for a few days a year. They might as well plant dandelions.

But he wasn't here for the garden. Looking around, there were just six units, and no upper floor. That meant the GPS marker had to be in the apartment at the back, the last one on the right. Slater strode over and pressed the doorbell. No one answered, and as he stood listening, no sound came from within. He pulled out his phone to photograph the name written on the little card above the bell: Bissiter.

Pulling open the screen door, he knocked loudly on the inner one. He already knew no one was home, but he wanted to get a look at the deadbolt. It was standard hardware-store equipment—that was very good news.

He let go of the screen, and it snapped back into place as he turned to walk back past the fountain. From the next doorway a reedy voice hailed him: "Can I help you?"

Slater paused to look. The form of a woman with short gray hair was visible behind the screen door. She was wearing a loud orange caftan.

"I doubt it," he said, "unless your name is Bissiter."

"She's in the apartment you just looked at. I don't think she's home. Is she in trouble? I bet you're after that boyfriend she had a while back. He certainly looked like trouble to me."

"I don't need the rundown on her degenerate sex life," Slater said. "How long has she lived here?"

"Who's asking?" the woman said, shifting on her feet.

"I'm an insurance assessor. I'm double-checking some things. What can you tell me about her?"

"I'm not going to tell you anything, unless you're carrying a badge."

"If that's your attitude," Slater snapped, "you can stop wasting my fucking time."

He strode out to the street and climbed into his car. On his phone he pulled up the location tracker for Conrad, his idiot cop ex-boyfriend. The drooling moron was at work, or at least his phone was, at the station in Slater's neighborhood. Slater sent him a text:

At your station? I'm coming over there.

Starting the engine, he pulled into the street and headed back downtown.

It was Conrad's own fault, letting him see the code that unlocked his phone. It wasn't really stalking, either—he needed to know where the idiot was sometimes, when he needed access to his cop resources. He'd installed the hidden tracker on his phone back when things had been good between them, when they'd agreed on everything, those long days when they'd been having fun. But that was all in the past.

Pulling up outside the station, Slater saw the text Conrad had sent in response:

I'm working.

He wrote back:

I'm here. Should I come in there and ask for you?

Slater had met some of his cop friends, so he knew Conrad wasn't embarrassed by his presence, but Conrad was aware that Slater could be unpredictable, and he wasn't about to let him stroll into his workplace—he'd come outside soon enough.

He climbed out of the Thunderbird and surveyed the yard next to the station. The city had replaced the turf with local dryland plants and open ground, and they'd done a good job of it. But why were they letting the live oak look like that? The damn thing was going to strangle on its own growth.

Conrad appeared at the entrance to the station, pushing through the doors and striding toward him, a striking figure in his dark-blue uniform. Barrel-chested even without his ballistic vest on, he had a square jaw, and thick dark hair, and a great body. Such a beautiful man.

"I have a job to do," Conrad said as he approached. "I'm not your personal manservant."

"That's not what you said back in the day. When I had my dick down your throat."

He put his hands on his hips and frowned. "You always say things like that. There's no need to be crass."

"I need some information."

"Of course you do. That's the only time I ever hear from you."

"What, you want me to call you and ask how your day was?" Slater demanded, stepping closer. "You're the one who dumped me, remember? The message was clear from the sole of your jackboot on my ass."

"I never kicked you."

"Metaphorically you certainly did. At least it freed you up to fuck your sweaty twinks."

Conrad rubbed his eyes and took a breath. "Metaphorically, Slater, what do you want?"

"I have an address, and I need to know who lives there."

"Text it to me. I'll see what I can find out."

Slater gestured to the tree in the yard. "You need to tell someone that the live oak needs pruning. It's in terrible shape."

As he glanced toward the yard, Conrad's brow furrowed. "The police don't actually do the gardening themselves."

"That's no excuse. That tree is miserable."

Conrad looked him over. "How is your sobriety plan going?"

"None of your damn business." Slater jabbed a finger at him and spoke through his teeth. "Not anymore." He turned on his heel and walked toward his car.

"Take care of yourself," Conrad called after him.

Who was he to be dispensing lifestyle advice? Idiot dick-smack Conrad. By the time Slater climbed behind the wheel, he was gone. Digging out his phone, he texted him the address of the apartment in WeHo, along with the unit number, and added:

The name on the doorbell is Bissiter.

Slater drove toward downtown, back to his

office. Upstairs there was no sign of Max. He swung his boots onto his desk, and pulled his keyboard into his lap. A cursory search for Marvel-Anne didn't reveal much. It appeared that she didn't spend time on social media, at least not using her real name. Everything that came up about her was related to *Sasquatch Search.*

When his phone buzzed in his pants, he pulled it out, glad to have the fruitless research interrupted. It was a text from Conrad:

> Only one name currently linked to that address: Sloane Bissiter.

The second text was an image, a portrait, with the familiar blue background of a driver's license photo. Sloane looked to be in her forties, and had dark hair. She was Filipina, maybe, even though her name sounded Anglo.

Sitting up, he searched online and found dozens of pages about a television producer with that name. There were photos of her too, at several red-carpet events, wearing a sparkly green off-the-shoulder gown at something called the Structured Reality Awards, and a plush burgundy dress at the Hidden Camera Awards. Her hair was up, and she was wearing a ton of eye makeup, but it was the same woman as in the DMV photo.

Looking through her industry credits, Sloane was the creator and producer of several television series. Going to all those red-carpet events had paid off—she'd won an award for Best Producer of a Daytime Tabloid Talk Show.

Based on all this, the woman looked like a civilian, not a lowlife. It was unlikely she was fencing stolen audio equipment. Maybe she was just a friend of Marvel-Anne. Based on her age, though, she was too old to be another sorority sister.

It was easy to track down her office phone number, and Slater dialed it. A voice-mail recording answered: "If you're calling about casting for *Ooh, No She Didn't,* leave your name and number."

"The name is Ibáñez," he told the machine, and rattled off his number. "I need to talk to Sloane Bissiter."

He'd barely had time to hang up and stretch before the phone rang. The caller ID showed it was the number he'd just dialed.

"Ibáñez," he said as he picked up.

"Were you calling about the wimpy boyfriend, or the security guard?" a woman's voice said.

"What? Are you Sloane Bissiter?"

"The boyfriend is already cast, but we still need security."

"If you'd stop talking, and let me explain—"

"I'm a busy woman, Mr. Ibáñez. The gig is tomorrow. Send me a head shot."

"I'm not going to send you anything, woman," Slater snapped.

"You know, you sound right. We'll give you a shot. Come in at nine. Wait—that's for the principals. Come in at eleven. Have you got a pen?"

No way was he going to audition for her like a damn trained monkey, but this sounded like a shortcut to a meeting with her.

"Where am I supposed to go?" he said, keeping his tone even. Sloane recited a street address, and Slater said, "Is that in NoHo?"

"Correct. See you at eleven." With that, the line went dead.

Staring at the screen on his phone as it faded to black, he thought it through. He could ask Andy to look into this woman, but maybe that was premature. He'd wait until he'd done some digging himself.

Keys rattled in the front door, and Slater locked his computer and got up. Max greeted him as he stepped in, wearing a dark suit with a yellow necktie, loose at the collar. He looked tired. Slater stood in the doorway to Max's office as he got settled behind his desk.

"How's your bigfoot guy?"

"It's progressing," Slater said. "I've got a couple of leads. What are you working on?"

"A window-shade job. I'll be stalking the alleged cheaters this evening."

Slater nodded. Infidelity cases were Max's bread and butter, and he seemed to enjoy the work. Slater hated those jobs—even if they didn't actually have to peep through bedroom windows, most of the time it felt like the client's goal was to punish their spouse for having sex.

"Can I borrow the Courier tomorrow morning?"

"Help yourself," Max said. "It should have plenty of fuel. Do you need it to transport a bigfoot?"

"I need to be a plumber."

"Then it's definitely the right vehicle."

Slater's phone buzzed, and when he pulled it out of his pants, he saw that it was Ryan. Stepping back into his own office, he picked up.

"What's going on?"

"I'm about to head back to the city," Ryan said. "I've got some news. Do you want to grab dinner?"

Slater told him the name of an eatery where they could talk, and added, "It's on Sunset."

"Let me put that in my phone," Ryan said, and a moment later, "Wow—the navigation says it'll take me an hour and a half. Does that sound right?"

"At this time of day, yeah."

Slater called good-bye to Max and went down to his car, then drove the few blocks to Broadway. There was enough time to visit Andy, a regular hookup who did some hacking for him once in a while. Andy refused to call it that, instead claiming that he did deep research. Regardless of what he called it, he charged underworld-scale fees for the work.

After he parked in a surface lot behind Andy's building, and paid the attendant the evening rate, Slater walked up the side street and rounded the corner. As he approached the entrance to Andy's building, he caught sight of a familiar figure. Lithe and with great hair, he stepped out of the lobby and walked the opposite way, up Broadway. Slater knew that guy—Kyle. The freaking little poser wanted to get with Andy. He'd even had the nerve to confront Slater about it.

Upstairs, he knocked on Andy's door and folded his arms while he waited. Andy had a wiry build and shaggy brown hair, and flashed a smile as he pulled the door open. When he was at home he usually wore boxer shorts and a tank top—his metabolism ran hot because of his CP.

Slater followed him inside. Andy's loft was one big room, with a bed and a desk and a compact kitchen counter. The multipane windows, a holdover from the building's former incarnation as a warehouse, looked over Pershing Square.

"Have you had time to wipe off your dick yet?" Slater demanded.

Andy frowned, his rhythmic random muscle

movements intensifying. "What are you … talking about?"

"I saw your boyfriend Kyle on his way out. I have to assume you're fucking him."

"He's not my … boyfriend," Andy said, and dropped into the chair at his desk. "And I'm not … going to talk about him."

"You don't have to say it. I know what's going on." Slater put his hands on his hips. "It's like I'm halfway with you. One foot in the door, the other outside."

"That's not my … doing. It's about you. I'm right here, right now." He threw up a hand. "Where are you? What do you … want from me?"

Slater glared at him, not able to answer.

"You want me not … to see Kyle?"

"I know that's none of my business."

"So why … are you angry?" Andy demanded. "You fuck other guys. This is typical … addict behavior. You want to have … all the compulsive sex you can get, and sleep with anyone you … want, but then I'm not supposed to."

"I'm not an addict," Slater snapped, and then closed his eyes for a moment. "I don't want to be angry with you."

Andy stood up and stepped close, putting his hands on his neck, his random muscle motion telegraphing into Slater.

"So don't be angry," he said softly.

Slater leaned in to meet his taut mouth, and spent a minute getting lost in it. Eventually he pulled Andy down onto the bed.

"Can we just cuddle?" Andy said, stretching out beside him. "I don't have enough … energy to fuck you."

"Kyle wore you out, huh."

Andy draped an arm across his belly. "Slater—stop talking."

SIX

Not long after, Slater woke to find Andy propped on one elbow, looking down at him, a faint smile on his face.

"What?" he demanded.

"You look so gentle when … you're asleep."

"I can't believe how tired I am."

"You don't seem hung over."

Slater scowled. "I'm not."

"It's not a criticism." Andy ran a hand over his shirt and massaged his chest.

"I have to go." Slater sat up and kissed him. "Bye, beautiful."

Out on the street, the daylight was fading, and he clicked on the Thunderbird's headlights once he'd started the engine.

In the parking lot behind the restaurant

where he'd sent Ryan, Slater spotted the Polara, and parked near it. The place served classic Mexican food and had 1940s-vintage red vinyl booths, wrought iron, and strings of colored lights. Stepping inside, it was crowded, but he spotted Ryan at a table, and walked over.

"How was the Polara?" Slater said as he sat down.

"Very red," Ryan said flatly. "It's hard to be subtle in a sixty-year-old hella red muscle car."

"It drives like a dream, doesn't it?"

"I have to admit, once you get used to it, it's a nice car."

Slater threw up his hands. "You're welcome."

The waitress came over, and Ryan ordered an enchilada. Slater asked for veggie fajitas, the only thing on the menu he could eat besides guacamole.

"Should we have a drink?" Ryan said. "What's good here?"

"Two margarita rocks," Slater told the waitress, who nodded before she stepped away, and to Ryan, "So what's your news?"

"I went to the bookstore. I didn't find Marvel-Anne's friend, but the guy working there thinks he knows who she is, based on the description Im Hae gave us. Her name is Norma López. He even knew where she works now. I can go back down there and find her tomorrow."

"You're going to put me out of a job."

Ryan laughed. "I do a lot of interviews for *Sasquatch Search*, so I'm capable of extracting information. I didn't even have to smash anything with a sledgehammer."

"It was a post maul."

"So what was at those GPS coordinates?"

"An apartment. The tenant's name is Sloane Bissiter. Does that sound familiar?"

Ryan shook his head.

"I've got a meeting with her tomorrow."

The waitress set down their margaritas, and Ryan clinked his against Slater's before taking a slurp. "Good choice."

After they'd eaten, Slater led the way out the back into the parking lot. The driver's door of the Polara hung open, and a guy in a khaki jacket was leaning inside.

"Whoa," Ryan said, and stopped short when he spotted the guy.

Slater strode over and grabbed his shoulder, pulling him out of the car, and slammed his back against it. He slapped his face, left and then right, a rapid kovac.

"What are you looking for?" he demanded, and slapped him again, then grabbed the collar of his coat.

The guy vainly pawed at his forearms, then tried to twist away. "Hands off, you jerk. That's my car."

Maintaining his grip, Slater called back to Ryan. "He doesn't have anything in his hands. Is anything missing?"

Ryan hesitated but then trotted over. "There was nothing up front. My bag is in the trunk." He leaned in the driver's door and flipped down the visor. "The paperwork is still here."

"Check the trunk," Slater said.

The guy tried to pull away again, and Slater gave him a shake and slammed him back against the car.

Hurrying around to the back of the Polara, Ryan lifted the trunk lid. "He didn't get my stuff."

Slater pulled the guy off the car and shoved him away, hooking a boot around his calf so that he'd tumble to the pavement. He got to his feet and adjusted his jacket, then stood there for a moment, glaring at him.

Slater advanced a few steps toward him, fists balled, and the guy quickly turned and loped toward the street. After watching him for a moment, Slater did a neck roll, trying to dispel the adrenaline, and then looked to Ryan.

"Did you lock it?"

"I might have forgotten. It's not like a modern car. You have to use the key."

Slater waved his arm. "It's a big city, man. There are sixty thousand homeless people around."

"That guy didn't look homeless," he said, and

slammed the trunk lid.

"He definitely smelled like it. If this car gets jacked, Duarte will put a hit on me."

"I'll be more careful. It's kind of a learning curve." Ryan ran a hand through his hair. "So where can I park it in your neighborhood?"

"We'll put it in my garage."

"You think there's room for it?"

"I know there is. Follow me."

Slater climbed into the Thunderbird and drove toward Westlake, cruising smooth and steady, signaling well before he changed lanes or turned a corner, and kept an eye on the Polara's distinctive headlights in the rearview.

Once his garage door rolled up, he pulled his car tight to one side and climbed out. The Polara sat idling in the alley.

Ryan rolled down his window and waved his arm. "I can't drive it in there."

"Let me," Slater said, and gestured for him to step out, then got behind the wheel. Once he'd eased the vehicle into the narrow space, there was just enough room to squeeze out the driver's door.

"Good thing you're not a hoarder," Ryan said, stepping inside. "Most people's garages are piled up with stuff."

Slater hit the button to roll the door down, then eyed Ryan. "Out in the woods you're calm, and level-headed, and fearless. A total badass.

Why are you worried about city stuff like parking a car?"

"If I break a branch off a tree, no one is going to break my kneecaps."

"Duarte's not really that guy. I shouldn't have exaggerated."

Upstairs in his apartment, Ryan's big backpack lay on the floor, and the sofa was still covered in sheets. Ryan flipped the top of the bag closed with his foot and turned to Slater.

"Can I sleep in your bed?"

Slater had to grin. "You may."

He balled up the sheets from the sofa and carried them into his bedroom, where he tossed them in the bottom of the closet. Ryan brought in his backpack and dropped it at the foot of the futon.

"So what do you do in the evening?"

"You mean my bridge group," Slater said, "and ladies' book club?"

Ryan chuckled. "I know you listen to top-quality podcasts, but you don't have a TV set."

"Well, you can't fuck a TV." Slater unbuckled his belt, then sat on the bed and untied his boots.

"So you want more sex from me."

"Much more. If you're up for it, that is. It's not a quid pro quo."

"I'm definitely up for it. Are you going to have your bourbon first?"

Slater pulled off his boots and rose. "The booze rules dictate that sex comes first. Otherwise things get muddled."

Stepping closer, Ryan put his hands on Slater's waist, and pushed his jeans down, and pressed into him. This guy was so beautiful, so responsive. His fingers in Ryan's hair, Slater leaned in and kissed him, feeling his burgeoning woody. As he sank onto the futon, Slater grasped his waist and pulled him down on top of him.

Ryan mouthed his neck, and his ear. "Do you take it as easily as you give it?"

"You can fuck me, Ryan, if that's what you want."

Ryan kissed him again and then got up, dropping his trousers and peeling off his shirt. Across his shoulders and curling onto his biceps was a tattoo in gradations of green and black, a stylized conifer forest that undulated with the contours of his skin.

Sliding off his jeans and his shirt, Slater watched as Ryan grabbed a condom, then climbed on the bed and spent a minute connecting with him, running his hands over Slater's body and nuzzling his neck. Slater grabbed his cock and squeezed, and when Ryan was rock-hard, rolled the condom on for him. With the lube Ryan massaged his way into him, then pushed up his knee and shoved his way inside.

Slater winced with the intensity of it, then relaxed into the rhythm as Ryan leaned into him, mouthing his neck and his ears, building up to pounding him, until finally he yelped, straining deeper, and came. Then Ryan stretched out beside him and grabbed his cock, and locked their mouths together, and stroked Slater until he came too.

Once he'd caught his breath, Slater got up and went to the kitchen, where he pulled the bourbon bottle from the cupboard and guzzled an approximation of his ration. He relished the burn, then coughed from the heady fumes. After he took a final pull from the bottle, he went back to bed. Ryan came in from the bathroom and lay beside him, his skin warm, and caressed his belly.

"This reminds me of my dad."

"You spent a lot of time in bed naked with him?" Slater said.

He chuckled. "Not the sex—the scent of the bourbon. Are you close to your father?"

"He died when I was a teenager."

"That must have been hard on you."

"It was pretty gross." Slater turned onto his side. The amber warmth was spreading from his belly, infusing his mind with the familiar mellow glow. As Ryan shifted, he caressed the forest inked on his shoulder blades. "I'm amazed at how vivid the green is."

"I guess there's no question about what it represents, or why I chose that graphic."

"When I listen to your work, this is exactly the image it evokes."

Ryan took his wrist and drew his arm across his chest, and Slater pulled him closer.

SEVEN

HEN SLATER WOKE, HE was alone, and spent a few minutes luxuriating in the bright daylight as he came to full consciousness. He got out of bed and went into the other room to find Ryan sitting on the sofa, fully dressed, working on his laptop.

"There's literally nothing in your icebox," he said. "I couldn't even find a soda cracker."

"I don't have any."

"So let's go out."

Slater frowned. "Give me a few minutes."

Having Slater work for him and sleeping with the guy didn't mean he couldn't go get his own damn breakfast. But it was Slater's own fault—he knew better than to stick his dick into his cases, but he'd done it anyway.

He washed up, and got dressed, and went back to talk to Ryan. "How does Middle Eastern sound for breakfast?"

"Perfect," he said, and folded his computer closed as he got up.

The brightly lit and sterile little place was close enough to walk, and they stepped in and ordered at the counter.

"Let's start with a triple espresso," Ryan told the clerk.

They sat by a window to eat, and as Slater was finishing his falafel, he watched a young guy walk in and approach the register. His dark hair was styled in an unctuous pomp, and he struck up an animated conversation with the clerk. Ryan was watching him too, he saw.

"He's fuckable," Slater said.

"That's not what I was thinking about."

"I'd steer clear—he's high. Although it's a little early for tweaker time."

"What's tweaker time?"

"When all the meth heads wake up from last night's binge. It's usually around two o'clock. They like to eat greasy stuff like quesadillas. It's why the restaurants in Boystown serve heavy breakfast food until mid-afternoon."

Ryan shook his head. "That's such an urban experience."

"There are lots of tweakers in the countryside.

The Mojave is full of them. I bet there are lots in Oregon too."

"But there isn't a daily calendar for their activities, and a dining culture built around them."

"You never lived in cities?" Slater said, and folded his arms.

"Not like this one. I lived in Crescent City, which isn't actually a city, and in Eugene. From there, Portland is the big smoke, but even Portland is a village compared to LA."

"Things work the same, though, don't you think? There's just more people here."

"That's probably accurate," Ryan said, "although Marvel-Anne always says Oregon is way whiter than California. I never really registered that."

"Of course you didn't. You're white."

"It's also easier to be anonymous in a bigger place. If you smashed up furniture with a sledgehammer in somebody's workshop in Eugene, everyone in town would know about it."

"I went for the sawhorse, not the furniture. And it was a post maul. Why is it so hard to remember that term?" Slater demanded. "Im Hae didn't get it either."

Ryan grinned and wiped his fingers. "So what are we doing today?"

"You should pursue your lead in La Mirada. See if you can track down Norma López. Call me if you need backup. Another thing—check in with Kawamura today. Ask him if he's heard from Marvel-Anne."

"What are you going to do?"

"I'll follow up with Sloane Bissiter."

"I feel like I'm paying you, but I'm doing half the work."

"That means it'll take half as long, and in the end you'll only have to pay me half as much. Besides, what else would you be doing today?"

Ryan nodded and got up, and they walked back to Slater's building, into the hallway on the ground floor.

"My bag is upstairs," Ryan said.

"You've got the key. I'll meet you at the cars."

Ryan headed up the stairs, and Slater hustled into his garage and went to the cabinet that sat just past the nose of the Thunderbird. It looked like a basic sheet-metal storage box from an office-supply store, but in reality it was heavily armored, and bolted to the wall, a safe hiding in plain sight—it was where he kept his sensitive tools and the illicit tech he got from the Russians in Glendale.

Once he got the doors unlocked, he pulled a vehicle tracker off its charger and closed the cabinet again. The tracker was a black plastic box, thicker than his cell phone, with magnetic ribs on one side. The power switch was a tiny recessed slider, and he clicked it on with a fingernail, then went to the Polara and stepped around the driver's side.

The car was parked tight to the wall, but there was enough room to squat at the rear tire and reach up into the wheel well. The magnets instantly found purchase—there was a lot of steel in these old vehicles—and it snapped into place with a satisfying tug.

As he stood up again, he heard keys in the door from the hallway, and Ryan stepped in, his bag slung over his shoulder. Slater watched as he set the deadbolt.

"Toss me your car keys," Slater said. "I'll back out the Polara."

Once he had it in the alley, he left it idling and stepped out. Ryan put his hand on the driver's door and then leaned in to kiss him. He went with it, but when Ryan pulled back, Slater had to chuckle.

"What's funny?" Ryan demanded.

"Nothing. I just didn't expect it."

Slater watched him shift into gear and pull away. That guy spent a lot of time off in the woods.

Back in the garage, he rolled the door down and then went to his tech cabinet to get his lock-picking gear—an electronic probe and a heavy binder with pages of numbered keys in little pouches. He put both into his red plumber's toolbox, then grabbed a pair of coveralls, and loaded it all into the trunk of the Thunderbird.

Max's place wasn't far away, in a bougie apartment building on Bunker Hill, looking down on the Civic Center. It seemed like a place for judges and politicians to stay during the workweek, but he had to admit it was close to everything, especially the freeways, and the security was tight.

At the front of the building were a row of eucalyptus trees, thriving in the hillside soil. Why did they plant those damn things? They were essentially an invasive weed that repelled the local fauna and sterilized the earth around them. He wouldn't want to live here if they ever caught fire either—they burned hot and relentless, like a road flare.

As he rolled up to Max's garage gate, he dug in the glovebox for the opener, then drove in and parked beside the little green pickup, a classic 1973 Courier. It had a few dents, and it could use a paint job, but the engine ran great. The agreement was that Max could drive the Thunderbird when Slater borrowed the Courier, but he never did, as he preferred his own car. It wasn't here— Max was out.

Once he'd transferred his plumber's box into the Courier, he pulled on the coveralls and his blue ball cap with the interlocking L and A sewn on the front, then grabbed a pair of black latex gloves from the box he kept in the backseat of his car and tucked them in the roomy pockets.

The Courier's tinny little engine started right away, and Slater revved it to climb up out of the garage and head toward WeHo. Sloane Bissiter said she'd be in Burbank by nine, and if she lived alone, as dumb-ass Conrad's text had implied, her apartment should be empty.

Slater parked out front and shifted the bill of his ball cap low over his brow, then pulled on the black latex gloves. The gate into the courtyard was ajar, as it had been yesterday, and he carried the plumber's box inside. As he passed the doorway where the woman had confronted him, he glanced over, but her door was closed.

At Sloane's apartment, he set down the box and then pulled open the screen door and knocked loudly. He listened closely, but there was no response, no sound within. Pulling out his phone, he reached into the plumber's box for the lock reader—a length of wire that connected to his phone with a key-shaped probe at the other end.

It was a great piece of tech that he'd bought from the Russians in Glendale, and even though Svetlana got him to pay a subscription fee to keep the software working, it was well worth it—it didn't get an accurate read on every lock, but it could read most hardware-store equipment, and that's what was on Sloane's door.

When he connected the probe to his phone, it launched Svetlana's app. The screen went black and displayed the word "готов." Stepping closer to the deadbolt, he inserted the probe. His phone went green and displayed a number: 435. Withdrawing the probe, he squatted at the plumber's box and opened the lid to lift the binder of keys just far enough to see the numbers on the pouches as he flipped through the pages. He found 435 and slipped it out, letting the binder drop back into the box.

Glancing behind him, the courtyard was empty. He took a breath and tried the key in the deadbolt. It twisted freely, and the bolt slid with a satisfying *thunk*. He pushed the door open.

"Maintenance," he called as he stepped inside, keeping his head down. No alarm sounded, and he closed the door behind him and did a quick scan for alarm tech. There was no alarm panel, no sensors on the door frame, no obvious cameras. Sloane must rely on her nosy neighbors to discourage burglars.

It was a one-bedroom place, with a kitchenette, he saw, and Slater quickly looked in the hall closet, and in the bathroom, pulling aside the shower curtain, and in the bedroom closet. There was no one here.

Flicking through the closet, he saw that the

clothes were women's, and in small sizes. He knew Marvel-Anne was tall and curvy—this stuff would never fit her. The bed was roomy enough for two, but it was unmade, and only one side was disturbed. There was only one toothbrush in the bathroom, and one towel—Sloane lived alone.

In the main room was a TV set and an audio receiver, but no sign of any pro equipment, nothing like what Ryan had shown him pictures of. If Marvel-Anne wasn't staying here, maybe it was just a business connection.

He'd learned all he needed to. Locking the door behind him, he carried the red toolbox toward the street, keeping his head down. As he passed the fountain, the sight of the stupid *Vinca* plantings made him scowl.

"Excuse me," a man's gravelly voice said. "What are you doing here?"

He was on the opposite side from the woman who had accosted him yesterday, in a different apartment. Slater ignored it and kept walking.

"Excuse me," he called, much louder this time.

Slater had no choice but to acknowledge him, and turned to where he stood in an apartment doorway. Affecting a high nasal tone with his voice, he said, "*¿Perdóname?*"

"Are you here to do the drains?" the guy said, and pointed to the sky. "The drains on the roof. *El piso.* They leaked last winter. *La lluvia,* you understand? I asked the landlord to send a plumber before it started raining. Is that you?"

Slater shrugged. "*No entiendo.* You should call to the lan'lord."

With that, he walked away. Even with his almost nonexistent Spanish, he knew that *piso* meant "floor," not "roof," so claiming not to understand the guy was completely legitimate.

He loaded the plumber's box into the truck and opened the driver's door, pausing to quickly pull off the coveralls before he climbed in. Once he was behind the wheel, he peeled off the gloves and scanned the sidewalk to make sure the tenant hadn't followed him, then started the engine and pulled into the street.

Not far away, in the center of Hollywood, was the mall at Highland Avenue, crowded with tourists day and night. Slater navigated the clogged streets around it and pulled into the underground parking garage. It stretched for acres and was always empty compared to the pedestrian bustle upstairs. Once he got up to the street, he dodged through the crowd and descended again into the adjacent metro station. As he got to the platform, the B Line train was pulling in, and he stepped aboard.

It took him under the hill to North Holly-wood in just a few minutes—much faster than he could ever drive it, even in the middle of the night. It was unlikely that he'd need an alibi, but if that nosy neighbor with the mangled Spanish fingered him for invading her apartment, he could claim he was already in NoHo waiting to meet Sloane.

Climbing the escalator out of the station, his phone showed that the address Sloane had given him was just a few blocks' walk. On the map it looked like a big complex—a TV studio, he realized.

When he got to the front desk, the security guard, a chunky guy in a dark jacket, seated behind a counter, gave him the once-over.

"I have an appointment with Sloane Bissiter," Slater told him.

"What series is she working on?"

"No idea."

He sighed wearily and turned to a computer screen, and clacked at his keyboard.

"She's on *Ooh, No She Didn't,*" he said finally, and pointed behind him. "Studio 7."

EIGHT

S LATER WALKED PAST THE guard's desk into the corridor and soon found the double doors with a big 7 posted above. Inside was a cavernous room, with walls painted matte black, and a constellation of stage lights suspended from the high ceiling. In the middle was an incongruous space decorated like an office, with a desk, a bookcase, and two upholstered guest chairs, all parked on a sprawling Persian carpet.

There were a lot of people around—some futzing with the electronics and the trio of cameras, some standing and talking. Stepping closer to the cameras, he saw that a set of bleachers sat at one side of the faux office. They must film with a live audience. Sloane's biography said she worked in reality television, but he had no concept of what this series was about. The set looked a lot like a shrink's office. And why was it so cold in here?

Scanning the crew, he spotted Sloane. Less glamorous today than in her red-carpet photos, she wore jeans and a dark blouse, and had her black hair hastily bundled up on her head. She stood near the desk, gazing at a tablet. Its blue glow illuminated her face, today nearly devoid of makeup, like in her DMV photo. Slater walked over and hailed her.

As she looked up at him, Sloane frowned. "Can I help you?"

"The name is Ibáñez. We spoke yesterday."

"You're late." She looked him over. "But you're perfect. You won't even need wardrobe. Just the shirt and a little makeup." She peered at his eyes. "Maybe some guy-liner. Do you know the drill?"

Slater put his hands on his hips. "I'm not interested in working for you. I'm looking for Marvel-Anne Willits."

Holding his gaze, she stood up taller. "I'm not interested in what you want. I'm trying to film an award-winning television program here, and we're about to let the audience in."

"Best Producer of a Daytime Tabloid Talk Show?" Slater said.

Sloane smiled. "So you watch."

"What do you know about Marvel-Anne?"

"We can talk about her, but it'll have to be

after the filming. You can either wait some-where off my set, or put on a shirt and stand by the bookcase and make a hundred bucks for two hours' work."

Slater glanced around the studio. He couldn't really press the issue right now, with all her col-leagues here, but he wasn't about to let her give him the bum's rush either. "What do I have to do?"

"I thought you watched."

"Refresh my memory."

Sloane sighed impatiently. "When a conflict breaks out on stage, you and Darnell step in to separate them. It's not a speaking part. Don't do anything until the stage manager tells you. She'll explain exactly when to intervene and when to back off. We'll have to get you an earpiece."

She turned to scan the studio, then shouted, "Darnell!"

A massive muscle-bound guy stepped over, and nodded to Slater, then eyed Sloane expec-tantly. His hair was in microlocs, and he wore a tight black T-shirt emblazoned with SECURITY in big yellow letters. Fuckable, Slater decided.

"Get him an earpiece, and show him the ropes," Sloane said, and walked off.

Darnell extended his meat hook of a hand. Slater told him his name as he shook it, and caught a whiff of his musky cologne.

"Have you ever worked as a bouncer?" Darnell

said. His tone was soft, incongruent with his imposing jacked body.

"I know how to defend myself."

"Well, this is much gentler than working with drunks. You won't have to throw any punches. The guests get into scuffles, but everyone knows the score—when you pull them apart, they'll let you do it."

"Who are these people?" Slater said. "Who goes on television to get into a dustup?"

"The program is called *Ooh, No She Didn't.* It's always a love triangle. Usually girl-boy-girl, like today, or two guys and a girl. Once in a while it's same-sex trios. Two of the guests always get into it, and sometimes all three."

Darnell gave him a few pointers about handling the brawls, and explained the format of the program.

"Whatever you do, don't say anything," he said finally. "You're just the muscle. And keep a poker face."

Slater nodded. "I get it."

"You need a T-shirt like mine."

Slater followed him to the side of the sprawling space, where a clothing rack stood next to a cart with some plastic tubs. Digging in one of the tubs, Darnell found a black T-shirt like his own, emblazoned with SECURITY in bright yellow, and tossed it to him. Slater unbuttoned his shirt and hung it on the clothes rack, then pulled on the T-shirt.

"You need a size smaller," Darnell said, looking him over. He stooped to dig in the plastic tub.

"This actually fits pretty well."

"It needs to show off your body."

The smaller version felt tight, but at least the fabric stretched, and it was long enough to tuck into his jeans.

"Better," Darnell said, watching him, and then flagged down a lavender-haired woman walking by. "Slater needs an earpiece," he told her.

"Of course he does," she said flatly. "It's not like everyone else is miked up already. Don't move—I'll be right back."

"I'll see you in there," Darnell said, and clapped him on the shoulder as he walked away.

A minute later the audio woman came back with a loop of wire in hand.

"Hold still," she said, and pushed something into his right ear, then looped the clip around the top. "We'll run the wire under your shirt," she said, and attached a little black box to the back of his belt. She untucked his T-shirt and reached under it, toward his neck. Slater could feel her hand and the wire snake down his back as she pulled it through.

"You're certainly not shy," he said.

She scoffed. "I don't have time for shy." She

tucked his shirt in again, then looked at the tablet she was holding and tapped at it. "Do you hear a tone in your earpiece?"

Slater pressed the device deeper into his ear. "Yeah, now I do."

"Hallelujah. You're new, right? Have you talked to the production accountant?"

"Where's he at?"

She pointed to a table in the corner. "Her name is Val."

Val was in her sixties, and rail-thin, and had a mass of gray-blond hair around her head. As he approached, she eyed Slater over a pair of half-lens reading glasses, and frowned.

"You're the new bouncer?"

"Correct."

"Sit for a minute," she said, and gestured to the folding chair beside her desk. "Are you legal to work in the United States?"

"Does everyone get asked that question," Slater demanded, dropping into the chair, "or just the brown people?"

Val scoffed and handed him a clipboard. "Fill this out."

It was a standard federal tax form, with just a few boxes to fill in. In the NAME field, Slater wrote a pseudonym he used sometimes, John Slade. No way was he giving these yahoos his real identity. Next to that he added a fake Social

Security number that he had memorized for situations like this. He wasn't sure if the number was connected to a real person or not, but he knew it would pass a cursory validity check.

When he handed the clipboard back to her, Val didn't even glance at it, setting it aside, and peered at his face, raising her chin to study him through her reading glasses.

"Sloane is going to scream if you don't see Arun."

Slater took a breath, suppressing an angry retort. "Who's Arun?" he said evenly.

"Makeup." She pointed to the side wall, where a guy sat on a stool next to an empty chair, absorbed in his phone screen. As he got closer, Slater saw that Arun had several portable cases open on the table beside him, loaded with bottles and brushes and sponges.

Arun was in his fifties, maybe, with his gray-streaked black hair in a pomp, and a matching bushy mustache. Looking up, he peered at Slater, studying his face.

"You'd better sit down."

As he took the chair, Arun adjusted a telescoping arm to bring the bright doughnut-shaped lamp at the end of it closer to his face.

Slater winced at the glare. "Go easy."

"Oh, honey," Arun said, affecting a Southern drawl. "Subtle is my middle name."

"Then you're in the wrong business."

Digging in one of his cases, Arun produced a stack of printed cards and held one up to Slater's cheek, then swapped it for another.

"I think you're a 7," he said finally.

"You haven't even seen me with my clothes off."

Arun cackled at that and turned back to his makeup case. "I mean your skin tone. I'm a 6, but you're a little darker." He clicked open a small box with brown makeup in it and wiped the surface with a sponge, then nodded to Slater. "Chin out."

As he dabbed the product on his jawline, then his forehead, Slater closed his eyes.

"Why is it so damn cold in here, Arun?"

"Standard studio procedure. Sweating looks ugly on camera, and sweat would ruin my work." He dabbed gently with the sponge, shifting to Slater's neck. "You have lovely skin. What products do you use?"

"Soap and water, sometimes."

"Then you're a lucky man. I should get your number. We'd make beautiful mocha-colored babies."

"I'm no scientist," Slater said, opening one eye, "but unless you've got ovaries, I don't think that's going to work."

"But I'd have a lot of fun trying," Arun said,

and chuckled at his own humor. "Keep your eyes closed."

Slater felt the tip of a tool running along his eyelid. "I bet you say that to all the boys."

"Open and look at the ceiling." Arun leaned in to work on his lower eyelids. "Don't take it personally. I flirt with everyone."

"I don't mind," Slater said, gazing at the black-painted joists high above. "I'll fuck you, Arun, if that's what you want."

"Your mother should have named you Frank. Maybe I will get your number." He stood back and studied his work. "Look down, then up."

"It's better if I take yours," Slater said, tilting his head upward. "I've got a lot going on. I'll call you when my schedule frees up."

"You're finished." Arun folded his arms. "Listen, bouncer—I'm not easy, and I'm not cheap."

"I guess I'm both. Suit yourself."

Slater stood up and walked toward the set. Darnell caught sight of him and nodded to call him over.

"We each handle the same person in every scuffle," he said, and gestured toward two women who stood near the desk, chatting amiably. "I've got the girlfriend, and you're on the hoochie mama."

They were both in their twenties, but it was obvious which one he meant—the girlfriend had on a prim pink sweater, and the other woman wore a slinky green halter top with no bra. She had a lot of eye makeup on, and garish lash extensions, and long straightened black hair.

"I guess she is a little hoochie," Slater said.

"Dude—it's not a judgment. That's her identifier in the script."

"There's a script?"

"It doesn't matter if you didn't read it," Darnell said quietly. "The stage manager will tell you what to do."

The woman in the sheer green top approached them, her stride languorous in spike heels. She was also wearing capri-length jeans—those, at least, were sensible.

"Who's my security?" she said.

Darnell put a hand on his shoulder. "This is Slater."

The woman flashed him a smile and extended a drooping hand. "Serena de Vere. It's a pleasure to work with you."

Slater grasped her fingers and gave them a delicate shake.

"Two things," she said. "Don't muss my weave."

"You mean your hair?"

"Correct. Don't even touch it."

"Fine by me," Slater said. "And the other thing?"

"I'll resist being pulled out of the fray, as the

script suggests, but when I extend my left elbow backward, that means you should forcefully extract me from it."

"Left elbow. Got it."

Serena raised her eyebrows, and dipped her chin. "Would you like to rehearse?"

"Nothing would give me greater pleasure, Ms. De Vere."

"You may call me Serena." She looked to Darnell. "If you'd be so kind."

Darnell seemed to know what to do, and stood in front of her. She grasped his forearms, like they were preparing for a martial arts sequence, and Slater stepped behind her, his hands extended at his sides, the way Darnell had shown him. Serena started struggling with Darnell, her hair flipping around wildly.

"Ain't nobody goin' mess with my man," she shouted.

Darnell's expression remained placid. Slater grabbed Serena's biceps and gave her a gentle tug, but she continued struggling, and Slater let it happen, keeping his hands on her. When her left elbow appeared, he grasped her arms and heaved her backward, taking a big step back so that she wouldn't crash into him. Serena flew out of her shoes and landed on her toes, and bounced once, catching her balance like a gymnast. When she turned to Slater, she smiled.

"You're very good, Mr. Slater."

"It's just Slater."

"Where did you study?" She leaned down to scoop up her shoes.

"That move was from middle-school wrestling."

"Well, I know I'm in good hands." Serena dipped her chin and fluttered her massive lashes before she strolled away, her strappy spike heels dangling from one hand.

"She's elegant," Slater said, leaning closer to Darnell. "And she enunciates so clearly when she's not doing the hoochie thing."

"Of course. She went to Juilliard. She's a consummate professional."

Slater folded his arms and eyed him sidelong, not asking the obvious question: then why is she doing this?

The lights went up on the set, and loud upbeat music started thumping. The crew had mostly cleared off, standing in the shadows on the sidelines.

"Looks like they're here," Darnell said, gesturing to the double doors behind the bleachers, propped open now.

He meant the audience, Slater realized, watching the string of people file in and start to climb onto the seats.

"Let me show you your mark." Darnell walked

over to the side of the faux office space, between the bookcase and one of the guest chairs, and pointed to the concrete floor just past the edge of the carpet.

"What's my mark?"

Darnell frowned. "It's where you stand when you're waiting to be called into a fight."

"I should stand by that little piece of tape?"

"On it, ideally." He glanced at the bleachers, slowly filling with bodies, and lowered his voice. "Keep in mind that someone is always watching you. Maybe even the camera. I try to project calm authority while I'm waiting."

Slater nodded and stood with his feet apart, hands folded over his belt buckle, the way cops and military people did when they didn't have a weapon in hand. Idiot Conrad called it the fig-leaf stance, but that probably wasn't an official title.

Darnell walked over to the other side of the bookcase and took a similar position, the pair of them visible to the audience and the cameras but on the sidelines.

In his ear, a woman's voice spoke. "Bouncer, if you're receiving, hold up three fingers."

That had to be the stage manager. Slater held up the requested digits for a moment, and looked around the studio, unsure of where she was.

"Thank you," she said, and his earpiece fell silent.

The people filling the stands looked like they were mostly college-age, some of them in small groups, chatting quietly. Once they were all seated, the music got louder for a moment, and a guy in a rumpled brown suit, holding a microphone, stepped onto the carpet in front of the desk.

"How's everybody doing?" he shouted into the mike, his voice booming and distorted through the sound system. Some of the audience clapped and called back to him. "I can't hear you," he shouted, and they clapped louder. "We're almost ready to go," he continued. "Is anybody here married?" he asked, and then proceeded to talk about his mother-in-law. He was telling a joke.

A stand-up comedian, Slater realized. He was warming up the audience, getting them amped up and vocal for the romantic carnage to follow. Before long he had them laughing and hooting, and then he wrapped it up and walked off, which earned him enthusiastic applause.

The music got louder and more frantic, the stage lights got dazzling bright, and the host stepped out. This guy looked like a shrink from central casting, with a little beard and round glasses, even a tweed jacket. The crowd seemed to recognize him, and screamed and clapped as he stood there, gesturing with his fists in the air, like he'd just won a prizefight.

Eventually he held up a hand and pulled a

stack of blue cards from his jacket, briefly consulting them. From his vantage point, behind the guy's right shoulder, Slater could see that they were blank.

"Neil never thought his girlfriend would find out about the other woman," the host said, and outlined some of the details of Neil's debauchery. Slater watched the audience, who sat in rapt attention. He only half-listened to the convoluted story, which somehow involved an archery class, and a stray arrow, and a fast-food parking lot.

Next the host introduced the man himself, and Neil came onstage and waved to the crowd. The guy was ferret-thin, and sallow, and had greasy hair. He looked like the kind of guy who'd get caught.

Neil sat in one of the armchairs, and the host spent a few minutes asking him questions about his love life, as the audience clapped and booed him in equal measures.

The host called for the girlfriend in the pink sweater, and when she walked onto the set, he introduced her as Linda. She sat in the other armchair, which Slater realized now was placed strategically far enough from Neil's that neither party could throw a punch without getting up first. She outlined her beef about Neil's infidelity, and for a minute or so she shouted at him, punctuated with wild gestures. Neil wouldn't meet her eye, and looked completely cowed.

When Serena appeared, everyone in the bleachers knew who she was, and greeted her with loud derision.

"I ain't need you," she shouted, addressing all of them by flinging her hands at them, all the while striding gracefully in her spike heels. She didn't get to sit down, as the only chairs were occupied by Neil and Linda. The host called her Eve, and asked her a few questions to elicit some belligerent responses from her. When the tension seemed to be heating up between the two women, Slater heard a calm female voice in his ear.

"Get ready to move."

Within seconds the girlfriend was out of her chair, and she and Serena started slapping each other.

"Step behind them," the voice said in his ear. "To the left."

As Slater moved toward them, Darnell came from the other side, stepping close to him.

"Not your left," the voice in his earpiece said. "The other left."

Slater moved to the right, behind Serena, and imitated Darnell's concerned expression and body language, his arms extended at his sides. Before they could pull them apart, the two women separated themselves.

"Back to your mark," the voice told him, as

Linda dropped into her chair, and Serena flicked her hair back with her fingernails.

The host continued to interview Serena, who proved to be a font of defiant smack talk.

"If she can't satisfy him," Serena said, holding up a well-manicured finger, "she needs to step aside."

Linda leapt out of her chair and started another slap fight. Slater's earpiece guide said, "Move in left and start to separate them."

Darnell used his arms to push them apart, but they leapt at each other again, slapping at first and then locked in a clinch.

"Pull her out, right about now," the voice said.

Slater moved in and grabbed Serena's shoulders, gently tugging her back. She ignored him, but after a moment, extended her elbow. Slater pulled her bodily out of the altercation. She let him do it, even though she continued writhing and screaming.

"He's already done with you," Serena cried, and then went limp in his arms.

"Back on your mark," his guide told him.

Serena found her footing again, and Slater released her, and went back to his position on the sidelines. It was hard to believe this was award-winning entertainment.

There was another slap fight, and Slater and Darnell moved in, but the women broke it up themselves before they had to put hands on them. Eventually the host stepped to the middle of the carpet and addressed the audience with a few pseudo-wise words to wrap things up, then waved emphatically with his hand high overhead. The music went up again. It was over.

It took a few minutes for the audience to file out, and then Sloane appeared on the stage.

"Thanks, everybody," she said, raising her voice. "This episode is in the can."

The crew cheered and clapped. Sloane paused to congratulate some of the other staff, and Slater waited near the set to keep an eye on her. He pulled out his earpiece and detached the box from his belt, then drew the wire out of his shirt, and piled it all on the unused shrink's desk.

As Sloane walked off the set, Slater followed her. She stopped to talk to a guy with headphones around his neck, but only for a moment, patting him on the arm, and then continued through a set of doors and into a hallway. Slater caught up to her as she stepped into a little office. It was crowded with file cabinets and thick manila folders stacked on every surface, even on top of the printer.

"You did great," she said, and dropped into the chair behind the desk. "Can you work again next week?"

"Where is she?" Slater demanded.

She waved a hand. "You said earlier you were looking for someone. Remind me who that is again?"

"Don't play coy with me," he said intently. "Marvel-Anne Willits."

"Was she a guest on the show?"

"She had some high-end audio equipment that came into your possession."

Sloane slowly shook her head. "I have no memory of that." She flashed a thin smile. "Sorry."

Slater pushed the door closed. "You've wasted hours of my fucking time. Do you have any idea how enraging that is?"

"What are you talking about?" she said, her brow furrowing. "You'll get paid."

Slater picked up a fat file folder from her desk and tossed it in the air. The bulk of it landed on the floor at his feet, but paper fluttered everywhere, into every corner of the little room.

"You fucking idiot," she shouted, and sat up. "Stop it."

"Most people try to use digital files these days," Slater said. "Less paper to deal with. Tell me about Marvel-Anne."

"I'm calling security."

"You hired me to be security, remember?" He slapped his palm on the bright-yellow label emblazoned on his chest.

Sloane reached for the phone on her desktop,

but Slater lunged for the receiver, and yanked it out of the base, snapping the wires. He tossed the handset into a corner, where it clattered to the floor.

"Sing, sister," he demanded.

Sloane pushed her chair away from the desk, bumping into the wall, her eyes wide. "I don't actually know Marvel-Anne," she said quickly. "I met her one time. She advertised online that she had some equipment to sell. I replied to her post, and she came by my apartment."

"Where's the stuff now?"

"In my storage unit. I bought it from her. I'm going to use it next summer on a project."

"What day did she come by your apartment?"

"It was last week." Her brow furrowed in thought. "Tuesday. I was home that day."

"Where did she advertise the equipment?"

"It's a site called In Da Biz LA. It's a market-place for industry people."

"Marvel-Anne's not in your industry," Slater said, waving an arm.

"She was using the account of a photogra-pher. I remember because I'd heard of the guy. He's done head shots for some of my actors. My guests, I mean. I thought it was odd that he had audio gear to sell, but it wasn't him who showed up, it was Marvel-Anne."

"Who is this guy?"

"He has a shop on Sunset. His name is Higgs."

"What else did Marvel-Anne tell you?"

"Nothing," Sloane snapped, and sat up. "How did you connect me to that woman? I only met her once."

"Did she tell you that the audio component has a location tracker built into it?"

"I didn't know that." Her brow furrowed. "You might actually be smarter than you look."

Slater held her gaze as he pushed a deep pile of folders off the top of a file cabinet. They landed on the floor with a *slap*, scattering a flurry of loose pages.

"You're a damn hothead, you know that?" Sloane said. "You need to get out of my office."

Slater eyed her for a moment. The dates lined up—Tuesday was when the device appeared in her apartment. He believed her, he decided.

As he pulled open the door, she shouted after him, "You'll never work here again."

That, Slater thought, was very good news.

NINE

AFTER HE'D RETRIEVED HIS shirt, Slater walked to the metro, and rode back to Hollywood, then drove Max's little pickup downtown and parked it under Max's apartment, next to his own car. Once he'd loaded the plumber's box into the trunk of the Thunderbird, he drove to his office.

The place was dark, and Max wasn't in. Glancing at the bony statue of Rey Pascual as he walked by, Slater went into his own office and dropped into his chair. It didn't take long to find the photographer named Higgs online. His self-portrait depicted a dark guy with a little mustache, his head shaved bald. That look worked for some guys. He was basically fuckable, Slater decided.

The content of Higgs's website implied that

head shots were his specialty, and as Sloane had said, he had a storefront on Sunset, on the Strip. When he found the office hours, they were vague and cryptic: "before and after golden hour, most nights until nine."

Slater searched for "golden hour," and found that it was a thing in landscape photography—the time before sunset when the horizontal yellow light provided good outdoor illumination. Higgs must consider himself an artist, not just a head-shot hack, if he was out with his camera every day for the lighting conditions.

A quick search told him sundown wasn't for several more hours. He'd go see Higgs then. In the interim, he had stops to make.

Sitting back in his chair, Slater pulled out his phone and looked at the tracker he'd put on the Polara. Svetlana's software always worked well, but the menus and labels were a clunky mashup of Cyrillic and distressed English. She and her brother had been here long enough to function in English, but he suspected they subcontracted the development of the illicit software to the motherland. The page for the tracker on the Polara said "работает," whatever that meant, but it also had a green checkmark, which meant it was working.

Right now the vehicle was parked in a lot next to the Natural History Museum. Scanning the list of its movements and corresponding map points,

Ryan had driven to a mall in Cerritos, not far from La Mirada, and spent a few hours, and now he was back in town. Why was he at a museum? Had he tired of his research, and decided to play tourist?

Locking his computer, Slater got up and went out to the front office, eyeing Rey Pascual as he flicked off the lights and left. He crossed the street to his car and drove to the freeway, then headed north, into hilly Mount Washington.

When he pulled into her driveway, he was glad to see only Doris's Buick. Her idiot boyfriend's car, a stupid midlife-crisis Boxster, was nowhere to be seen. It simplified things—if that guy wasn't here, Slater wouldn't be tempted to punch him in the face.

As he killed the engine, his phone buzzed with a text from Ryan:

Are you around?

Slater texted him Doris's address, and added:

Come into the backyard, through the gate on the left side.

From the trunk of the Thunderbird he pulled on a pair of work gloves, then took the bag of seed he'd bought and carried it around the side of the house, through the gate and into Doris's backyard.

He dropped the bag on the plot he intended to plant, then grabbed some tools from the shed. Doris stepped out the back door of the house. Petite in stature, these days she was letting some gray show in her dark hair. Today she was wearing jeans with a gray sweater.

"You're here to do the mulch?" she said, walking over to him.

"And plant for spring." Slater rested the head of the rake on the ground.

Her eyes narrowed. "Are you wearing guyliner?"

"I guess I am." He'd forgotten about Arun's handiwork at the studio.

"You haven't done that since high school."

Slater waved dismissively. "I thought we'd try California poppies this year."

"I love those," she said. "They're so pretty."

"Unfortunately you won't see them bloom until April. I also brought the sweet peas you wanted."

Doris smiled. "Even though you think they're inappropriate."

"They're too sentimental, and ephemeral. But I know you love them."

"You've given me roses for every season," she said, gesturing to the rosebushes across the yard. "You can't tell me they aren't sentimental."

"Roses don't mess around," Slater said. "The

prickles say, 'Don't grab me,' and the buds tell you, 'I've got something to show you soon.' And then *bam*, a straightforward dramatic bloom—take it or leave it."

Doris laughed. "And sweet peas?"

"They say, 'Well, I'm going to sneak around over here, and there may be some color later, but you'll have to watch for it.' And then, 'Wait, is it too hot? Too dry? I'm just going to collapse now.'"

"Well, I hope they can get along with the roses."

"You have a piece of lattice in the shed," Slater said, absently tapping the rake on the earth. "I'll wire it to the fence and plant them there. You'll be able to see them from the kitchen."

"That sounds perfect." Her expression became serious. "Did you remember your father's birthday is Friday? I wanted to plant a *Plumeria* for him."

"Why a *Plumeria?*"

"I read that it's used as a memorial in Latin America."

"It's going to need well-drained soil."

"Maybe the high ground?" Doris said, and gestured to the side of the yard.

"That'll work. Do you want me to find one?"

"You'll make out better than me," she said, and squeezed his arm, then went into the house.

Slater pulled the wire fence off the mulch pile and spent some time with the rake spreading it on the various plant beds. After that he carried the sheet of wooden lattice over to the fence. It was old, and its interlaced laths were sagging a little, but that wouldn't show once the pea vines grew onto it. He lashed it to the fence posts and then planted the peas. Next he moved on to the bed of poppies.

As he was massaging the seeds into the soil, Ryan called to him.

"Look at you, up to your elbows in dirt."

"The story of my life," Slater said, and sat back on his heels.

Ryan stood there with his hands in his pants pockets, beaming at him.

"What?" he demanded.

"It's just interesting to see a different side of you."

"I have to get my hands dirty once in a while. Reconnect with the earth."

"Tell me about it," Ryan said. "In this endless city you'd need that. For me it's when I hike into the woods. A few minutes away from the car, and I start to feel like my batteries are getting recharged. Like I'm becoming whole again."

"It sounds like the same kind of experience."

He frowned. "Are you wearing makeup? I didn't see anything like that in your apartment. I was surprised you even had a toothbrush."

"It's from when I talked to Sloane Bissiter

today. She met Marvel-Anne online. Your partner sold her that audio equipment."

His face clouded. "So she kyped it."

"What does that mean?"

"It wasn't hers to sell. What did Sloane say about Marvel-Anne?"

"Nothing. It was a brief business transaction. Marvel-Anne went to her place last Tuesday. I'm pretty sure she's telling the truth—that's the same day the GPS data said the gear appeared in her apartment."

"How is that connected to you wearing guy-liner?"

"We'll get into it later."

"Your mother is delightful, by the way," he said, gesturing toward the house.

Slater scowled. "I told you to come through the side gate. You didn't need to bother her."

"She's making us dinner."

"Damn it," Slater muttered. "Of course she is. Why did you have to go and stir that up?"

"I didn't stir anything up." He frowned. "She was in the driveway."

Slater scoffed. "Did you find Norma López?"

"She works at a shopping mall now. One of those kiosks. She sells cell-phone accessories."

"What mall?"

"I forget the name, but it's a big one. In Cerritos," Ryan said, pronouncing it "*ser*-ih-toes."

"It's 'ser-*ee*-tos.' Did you talk to her?"

"She couldn't really avoid me, working out in the middle of the mall."

Slater gestured impatiently.

"Norma says she knew Marvel-Anne back in Fresno. She hasn't talked to her in a long time. I told her to call me if she heard from her. I gave her my number."

"Did you believe her?"

"I think so. I guess we'll see if she calls."

"I can drop in on her myself," Slater said, "and apply some pressure, if you think there might be more."

"I've seen you do that. I'm not sure it would work in such a public setting."

"You just came from there?"

"Right," Ryan said, and looked away, shifting on his feet.

It would have been obvious he was lying even if Slater hadn't known about the museum. There was no point in confronting him about it, he decided. He'd been forthright about the part of his day that mattered, and what he'd said about his travels jibed with what the tracker showed.

"You know, Im Hae made it sound like Norma was foxy," Ryan said, "but she's not all that. Although she was wearing a miniskirt."

As Ryan described Norma and related their conversation, Slater went back to planting the poppy seeds, on his knees to massage them into the soil. Ryan talked about driving the Polara, and how it handled on the freeway, although he called it "the interstate." He asked again why Slater was wearing guy-liner, and Slater explained the work he'd done on Sloane's television program.

Eventually Doris came outside. "Are you ready to eat?"

"I just need to mulch this bed," Slater said, rising to his feet, "and water everything. Then we'll come in."

"You missed some spots over there," Doris said, gesturing across the yard at some patches of bare earth. "Did you not have enough mulch?"

"Those are for the bees. Some of our native species need open soil."

"See how lucky I am, Ryan?" Doris said. "I have my own personal horticulturist."

"I'm just a part-time gardener," Slater said, and picked up the rake.

"But you know your stuff. My yard always looks like a million bucks." She gestured toward Ryan. "Did you know that Ryan's father was Jewish?"

"How long were you two in there conspiring?" Slater demanded.

"We were having a chat," Doris said. "Not cooking up a rebellion."

Ryan grinned. "It wasn't all that long."

Slater glared at them both, and went back to scattering the mulch. Doris went inside, and Ryan stood nearby, chatting about the garden work. After Slater soaked the new plantings, he drank from the hose, then pulled off his gloves, and they went inside. At the table in the dining room, Doris served them each a bowl of barley soup and a plate of string beans.

"I couldn't think of anything else to make for the vegan," she said, gesturing with her spoon.

Between bites, Slater said, "This is perfect."

"Is your son high-maintenance?" Ryan asked her.

Slater shot him a look, and Doris just shrugged.

"I've gotten used to it." She eyed Ryan. "So, can I ask what you hired Slater to do?"

"That's privileged information," Slater said.

"So secretive." She sighed. "What do you do for a living, Ryan?"

"I run a podcast called *Sasquatch Search*. We look for bigfoot."

Doris's eyebrows shot up. "You actually go out into the forest?"

"All over the country."

"Have you ever found one?"

"We've seen lots of evidence," he said, "but we haven't had in-person encounters. Not yet, at least."

"And you can make a living at that?"

"So far."

"Well, if anybody can find the bigfoot, you seem like the kind of guy who could."

She rose and stepped into the kitchen, returning with three bowls of fruit—sliced Asian pears and blueberries.

"The great thing about your generation," Doris said, eyeing Ryan as she sat down again, "is that you'll likely go through several careers. The world changes faster now than it used to."

"You don't think *Sasquatch Search* is a lifetime job?" Ryan said, a smile playing on his lips.

"Maybe it will be. Who knows?" She shrugged. "But I've been kicking around this planet for many decades, and I know that things can start to look different in a very short amount of time. So stay flexible." She waved a hand. "Be light on your feet. Don't be afraid to embrace the next challenge."

"Stop trying to mentor him," Slater said, gesturing with his spoon. "He's a grown man."

"And I'm a grown woman," Doris said, reaching over and squeezing his forearm. "Don't tell me what to do."

"It's actually a valuable perspective," Ryan said, and to Doris, "I appreciate the wisdom in your words."

"She used to be a teacher," Slater said.

Ryan nodded. "We talked about that."

Slater gritted his teeth and eyed them in turn. Why did it feel like they were up to something? It was his own fault, telling the guy to come over here.

After they'd helped Doris clean up, she walked them to the front door.

"Good luck with your mysterious project," she said, "whatever it is."

Slater paused on the step, and leaned in to kiss her. "Love you."

Ryan thanked her, and then pulled Doris into a quick embrace before he followed Slater out. The Polara was parked at the curb, red and luscious in the warm fading daylight.

"So you got a lead from Sloane?" Ryan said, pausing in the driveway. "Should I come with you?"

"I'll tell you about it after." Slater pulled open the door of the Thunderbird. "I need to get there soon."

"Do you mind if I go to your place? I feel like I need a nap."

"You don't have to ask. That's why I gave you the key."

TEN

S LATER CLIMBED INTO HIS car and backed into the street, nosing around the Polara and then heading toward the freeway. Twilight was fading by the time he got to the Strip, and he parked at a meter a few doors down from Higgs's photo studio. This wasn't really the Strip, he realized. It was farther east, a seedy commercial stretch of Sunset.

The sign in the door to Higgs's shop said CLOSED, but when Slater pushed on it, it swung open. It looked like a retail place, with an extensive collection of black-and-white portraits on display behind the counter. It wasn't a regular wall of fame with autographed photos of celebrity clients; this was the product—head shots of actors. On the opposite side of the room were a couple of umbrella lights on stands and a chair in front of a pale blue backdrop. Maybe a setup for passport photos.

A guy stepped out of the back room and frowned at the sight of him. He was still bald, but he'd lost the mustache—this was Higgs. Not as tall as Slater expected, he was wearing dark chinos and a kente-cloth vest over a white T-shirt.

"We're closed," he said firmly.

"I'm not here for your casting couch," Slater said. "Tell me about Marvel-Anne."

"What about her?" Higgs grabbed a camera from under the counter, a pro SLR with a long lens, and briefly peered through the eyepiece.

"When did you see her last? Where is she right now?"

Higgs set the camera down and sighed impatiently. "I have a gig to get to."

"Answer the question," Slater demanded.

"My clerk blew me off, which means I'm working on my own—I don't have time for you right now. Unless you can run an SLR."

"That one?" Slater said, pointing to the camera he'd laid on the counter. "It's mostly automatic. A monkey could run that camera."

"You know photography?" Higgs said, eyeing him.

"I don't run a head-shot factory, but I'm no tyro."

"That's great. Help me out right now, and afterward I'll give you all the time in the world."

"Is there a labor shortage or something? I'm not interested in working for you."

"I'm leaving now. You can either come back in an hour, or walk up the block with me and take some pictures."

Slater ran a hand through his hair and stifled a sigh. "Golden hour is over. What are you photographing?"

Higgs beamed and grabbed another camera, a similar pro job with a heavy long lens, then stepped around the counter, handing one of them to Slater. "I'll explain on the way. Let's go."

He hustled Slater out the front door of the shop and hurriedly locked it. On the sidewalk he headed west, walking fast. Slater matched his stride.

"Is this fully digital?" Slater said, looking over the camera.

"Just focus it and press the shutter button."

He looped the strap around his neck, and under one arm, then twisted the camera onto his back.

"How do you know Marvel-Anne?"

"We'll talk about that after," Higgs said. "Tonight is all about Artémise. The Fates have smiled on me. She's staying at a hotel right up the street."

"She's that pop star?" Slater said, trying to place the name.

Higgs looked at him askance. "She's *the* pop star."

"So you're a paparazzo."

"I'm a photographer," he said firmly, stepping sideways to avoid an oncoming foot scooter.

"How do you know you'll be able to see her tonight?"

"Her agent put out the word. She'll be stepping out the front door and into a limo in just a few minutes."

"Why would she advertise that?"

"It's how the game works," Higgs said. "She gets publicity while pretending she doesn't want it. Knowing when the cameras will be out gives her a chance to curate an outfit and get her makeup right."

"And you get to take not quite candid photos of her."

"You know how to run that camera," he said, breathing hard now, "but do you know how to shoot tag-team?"

"You'd better explain it to me."

"We stand on opposite sides of the door. When Artémise comes out, I'll yell her name. If she looks at me, I get the full-face shot, but if she turns away, it'll be toward you, and you'll get the shot."

Walking up on the hotel, there was already a small crowd on the sidewalk. Most of the people had serious cameras like Higgs, but a few of them looked more like fans.

"What does Artémise look like?" Slater said.

"How can you not know that?"

"Because it doesn't freaking matter." He waved a hand. "Maybe I've seen her. I can't remember."

"You'll know her when you see her," Higgs said. "Artémise is luminous and otherworldly. She has an intense aura." He gestured to the hotel's doorway. "You take the right flank."

Higgs strode across to the opposite side, and Slater took a position a few yards back, and planted his feet apart to make it harder for these idiot fans to jostle him—he knew they'd freak out when the pop star appeared. He hoisted the camera to his eye and looked through the lens, twisting the focus ring and snapping a couple of test shots. How did he let himself get roped into this? For the second time today he was working for a deadbeat.

A vehicle pulled up at the curb. The limo, Slater realized. It was white with dark tinted windows, and more like a roomy town car, not really a stretch job.

Standing next to him, another photographer, a chubby guy with unkempt hair and a week's stubble, holding a camera with an expensive-looking long lens, leaned closer. "Why do black people always have white limos?"

Slater eyed him and frowned. "What?"

"Didn't you ever notice? The country-and-western awards is all white folks, and they show up in black limos. The R&B awards is all black folks, and they show up in white limos. And here's Artémise's white limo."

"I've never covered those events," Slater said, but the guy was ignoring him now, instead focused on the hotel lobby, his camera up and at the ready.

Through the glass Slater could see a bustle of activity inside. The fans pressed closer, some of them starting to scream, as a trio of burly guys in dark clothing stepped outside. It was obvious who Artémise was, walking just behind them with another woman. Two more bodyguards followed behind. She was tall, and wearing a white jumpsuit with pink sunglasses, even though it was dark out. Her tight Afro was from another era, but given her fame, she was probably single-handedly bringing it back into style.

Artémise paused on the sidewalk, her comparatively drab companion and the guards stepping away from her, giving her space to be seen. She smiled beatifically, looking right and then left as people shouted her name. The bodyguards kept an eye on the fans, warding off the few who tried to get too close.

On Max's window-shade jobs, Slater had worked with cameras often enough that he knew what he was doing, knew how to frame the target. Adjusting the zoom lens, he took a dozen or so shots—some of the whole outfit, some from the waist up, and a couple of close-ups, catching Artémise as she looked right at him, a smirk curling her glossy lips.

A minute later, the posse continued toward the limo, with the bodyguards clearing the path. The starlet and her companion and a couple of the guards climbed in, and the vehicle pulled away. The intense energy of the moment quickly faded as the fans started to disperse. Slater scanned the crowd for Higgs, who caught his eye and nodded down the street.

Slater caught up with him farther along the block.

"Isn't she glamorous?" Higgs said. His eyes shone, and a smile was plastered on his face— the guy was still starstruck, still high from the experience.

"She's definitely managed to create an atmosphere around herself," Slater said. "I don't know if I'd call it otherworldly."

"You're jaded." Higgs waved a hand. "Indifferent, like so many Angelenos. Singed and blinded from standing too close to the flame of glamour."

"I grew up in this town," Slater said, "but not anywhere near your industry. I'm not jaded—I'm just not interested in what that woman has going on."

"She's not a woman," Higgs said flatly. "She's Artémise." He waggled his fingers for the camera Slater was carrying. "Let's see what you got."

As they walked back toward his shop, Higgs studied the screen on the back of the camera, and flipped through the images.

"You have an eye," he said finally, stepping up to the door of his business. "I think you got some decent shots."

"I need to get paid if you use any of mine," Slater said, following him inside.

"Sure—I'll let you know." He went to the counter and set down the cameras.

Slater put his hands on his hips. "I'll be watching the stock photo sites. I know exactly what my shots look like. Don't even think about trying to screw me out of the royalties."

Higgs's eyebrows shot up. "OK, boss. Who are you, anyway? I didn't even get your name."

Slater dug in his hip pocket and produced a business card, handing it to him.

"You're in insurance?" Higgs said, scanning it. "Why are you looking for Marvel-Anne?"

"That's not how this is going to go. You just wasted an hour of my time on some diva with a marketing team. Now you're the one who's going to sing, brother."

Higgs frowned. "I don't think I'm going to tell you anything."

Slater lunged for him and struck him hard with his palm, right and then left, a rapid kovac. Higgs stumbled back against the counter, holding his cheek.

"Get the fuck out of my store," he shouted.

Rushing him again, Slater batted his forearms away. Why did people always make the same defensive move, holding their arms up like that? It's almost like they wanted to get smacked. He delivered another slap and grabbed a fistful of Higgs's T-shirt.

"How do you know Marvel-Anne?" Slater said through his teeth.

Higgs pawed vainly at his wrists, but then gave up as Slater pressed into him, grinding him back into the counter. Panting and trying to lean away from him, there was fear in his eyes.

"College," he said. "We dated in college."

"Which one?"

"Fresno."

"Where is she?" Slater demanded.

"I heard she was in town," he said quickly, "but I haven't seen her."

"Who told you she was here?"

"Marvel-Anne did herself. One short phone

call. A week or so ago. She wanted to use my In Da Biz account to sell some junk online." His eyes narrowed. "Have you got a stiffy right now?"

Slater studied his face. "No."

"Yes, you do."

"Are you into it? Lock the front door. You can smoke me right now."

"I'm married," he said, raising his voice.

"To a woman, right? When's the last time she went down on you?"

"Dude—that's so inappropriate."

Stepping back, Slater let go of his shirt.

Higgs scowled at him as he tugged on the sides of his vest and flapped them into place. "What the hell is wrong with you? You got turned on from hassling me."

"No one is hassling you." Slater lifted the camera he'd been using from the countertop and switched it on, illuminating the back screen. "You're going to have to give me more, Higgs. I'd hate for you to lose all these pretty pictures of the great and wise Artémise."

"Put that down," he snapped.

"I don't even think there's a trash folder on this thing," Slater said, scrolling through the photos. "It'll just delete them forever, won't it?" He met Higgs's gaze. *"Poof."*

"I don't know where she is," he shouted, and put his palms on his bald head, his face contorted with anguish. "You have to believe that."

"She was your college girlfriend, and you don't know anything about her? Can you see why that's hard for me to believe?"

"Did you look into the fracking?"

Slater frowned. "What does that mean?"

"Marvel-Anne had a meeting." He snapped his fingers. "I remember. She got her degree in geology, right, but you knew that already. She had a meeting with an oil company. Let me check my phone."

"No tricks," Slater said, waggling the camera and watching him closely. "Why do you have her agenda on your phone?"

"I don't—when we talked she said she was driving, and asked me to look up the address so that she wouldn't have to pull over." Higgs peered at his phone, and thumb-typed a few characters. "It'll be in my search history." A moment later, he grinned. "Here it is—McInnes Shale Oil. It's in Long Beach."

"Show me." Slater set the camera on the counter and took Higgs's phone, then pulled out his own phone and photographed the listing on the screen.

"That's something, right?" Higgs said.

"Call her now," Slater said, handing his phone back.

Higgs's lip curled into a sneer, but he dialed,

and then set the phone on the countertop. After a few rings, Marvel-Anne's familiar voice spoke—her voice-mail greeting.

"Hang up," Slater said. "If she calls you back, find out where she is, and call me. You've got my number."

"She's not going to call back."

"You can send my photo royalties to that number too." Slater met his gaze. "If you hold out on me, I'll come for you."

He turned and walked out to the street. Once he was out of Higgs's view, he grabbed his crotch to adjust his junk. Higgs was right—it was messed up to get turned on by a straight guy when he was interrogating him. But the guy was hot, and smelled fresh, and there was that bald head.

Once he was in his car, Slater texted Ryan:

Still at my place?

His reply came soon after:

I never made it. I'm in Pershing Square.

Slater wrote back:

Meet me at the bar in the Baltimore Hotel. It's right across the street.

Before he pulled out, he checked the vehicle tracker on the Polara. It was parked in the garage under Pershing Square. So at least that was true.

The timeline before that was spotty, as the device didn't always get a clear sense of where it was. It relied on Wi-Fi signals rather than the precision of GPS. The advantage was that it used way less power, and would operate for a lot longer, and it didn't need a view of the sky, but Svetlana's software couldn't always interpolate a physical location from Wi-Fi signals. Based on the time that it appeared in that garage, though, Ryan had probably gone there directly from Doris's place.

ELEVEN

N OT LONG AFTER, SLATER walked into the bar at the Baltimore. It was a century-old classic, with mahogany and stonework framing the long bar. Ryan was perched on a bar stool, his hand on an almost-full glass of draft. Slater climbed onto the stool beside him.

"Hey, buddy," Ryan said, and flashed him a smile.

"Did you know Marvel-Anne is a geologist?"

His eyes grew wide. "Yes, I did."

The bartender stepped over, and Slater pointed to Ryan's beer. "A small of whatever that is." As the guy walked away, Slater dug out a twenty and set it on the bar top.

"Why does that matter?" Ryan said.

"I'm starting to feel like I'm getting the

runaround," Slater said intently. "TV people, and Artémise, and now the goddamn oil industry."

"Artémise? Slater, I don't know what you're talking about."

"Why didn't you tell me she's a geologist?" he demanded.

"I didn't think it was relevant." Ryan matched his volume. "She doesn't work as a geologist. I don't know if she ever worked in that field. I told you she went to grad school, but you never asked what her degree was in. Did you think it was in Sasquatch studies? That's not a thing. Not yet, anyway. I have a degree in English lit—do you need to know that?"

"You need to tell me everything. Otherwise I'm flying blind." He paused as the bartender set down his beer and whisked away the twenty. "Have you heard of a company called McInnes Shale Oil?"

"No," he said emphatically.

Watching him closely, Slater decided he was telling the truth.

"How is that connected to Marvel-Anne? And what does Artémise have to do with it?"

He lifted his glass and tapped it against Ryan's, and took a long drink, then told him about meeting the photographer.

"Here's to Artémise," Ryan said, and hoisted his glass. "I did what you said, and texted Kawamura. He said he's heard nothing from Marvel-Anne."

"Show me." Slater took his phone and scrolled through the short text exchange.

"After he said that, I looked at his social media. He posted a weird photo."

Slater handed his phone back. "Weird, how?"

"He told me before that he was headed to Seattle, but it doesn't look like Seattle. There are palm trees." Ryan swiped at the phone to find the image, then handed it over.

It was a selfie of Kawamura, wearing sunglasses and a T-shirt, sitting at a table with a stubby bottle of beer, a brand he'd never seen before. Behind him was some foliage, and beyond it the beach, and a stretch of ocean. Those trees. Slater zoomed in on the photo, studying the palms in the middle distance.

"That's here," Slater said. "In Venice."

"Seriously?" Ryan took the phone back and scowled at the screen. "That bastard lied to me."

"If he posted that, he's not hiding his whereabouts, so he's not lying low. But it does seem odd that he didn't mention he was here—especially if he knows you're in LA too."

"Of course he knows. Omitting the truth is lying too. I'm going to call him."

"Don't," Slater said. "Text him and ask directly, 'Are you in LA?' If he says yes, insist on getting together. I'll take a run at him."

"He carries a firearm. I don't think you want to mess with this guy."

"I meant that I'd interview him."

Ryan took a breath, and spoke more calmly. "Do you think Kawamura is relevant?"

"All three of your team are in town right now. Doesn't that strike you as significant? And why did he let you think he was in Seattle? He's hiding something."

"Maybe he just doesn't want to see me."

"That's possible. But it might be more than that."

Ryan nodded. "I'll text him." He spent a moment thumb-typing on his phone, then tucked it away and sipped his beer. "You know, it's been a few days, but I have the feeling that Marvel-Anne is still around."

"Is that based on any additional evidence you haven't told me about?"

"It's just a feeling. A psychic insight."

"Well, if you psychically get a street address, let me know—I'll drive you there."

"I can't believe you saw Artémise tonight," Ryan said, his tone brightening. "What was she wearing?"

He had to think about it. "A white one-piece. Like a flight suit."

Ryan gazed at his phone and tapped at the

screen. "Like this one?"

Slater glanced at the photo. "That's online already?" He took the phone and looked closer. "I might actually have taken that shot."

"It's easy to check the photo credit." Ryan took the phone back and tapped the screen. "Whoa—you did take it. It says 'S. Ibáñez for Higgs Photography.' It's nice that Higgs is being honest about it."

"He wouldn't be if I hadn't told him he had to pay me."

"This is one of the top gossip sites in the country. I wonder what they pay for photos like this?"

"A few hundred bucks, I think," Slater said. "The real money comes when it gets used a lot. I doubt that it will—there were a lot of other cameras there tonight."

When they'd finished their beer, Ryan said, "Where's your car?"

"Under the square."

"That's where the Polara is too."

Slater slid off the stool and gathered his change, leaving a couple of singles for the bartender. Once they got to his place, he spent a minute parking both vehicles in his garage.

"You know, you're very sweet with Doris," Ryan said, as they were climbing the stairs.

"I don't really have a choice. She's my mother."

"I don't even hug my mother anymore."

Slater eyed him as he unlocked the door to his apartment. "That's the most goyische thing I've ever heard."

"Well, she is a Protestant." Ryan chuckled. "Doris thinks you're the best. The sunrise and the sunset and all the daylight in between."

"I am her only offspring. Plus she's always been a little delusional."

Ryan set his bag on the sofa and stood facing him, his eyes soft, intent. Slater knew that look—the deepening interest, the idealizing, the infatuation.

"I'm not the best anything, Ryan," he said quietly, holding his gaze. "I'm trouble."

"I can see that too."

Slater turned away. Stepping into the bedroom, he crouched to untie his boots, then pulled off his shirt. Ryan followed him in, and dropped his trousers, folding them neatly, like he goddamn lived here, then started to unbutton his shirt. Slater was getting sick of having the same guy in his bed every night. But he had to admit, it could be worse. Ryan was hot, and innocuous, and into it.

As Slater unbuckled his belt, Ryan said, "Stop for a second."

"What?" he demanded.

"Why are you wearing a security T-shirt?"

"It's from *Ooh, No She Didn't*. I thought it might be useful someday."

"They gave it to you?"

"Let's just say it's mine now."

"It makes you look tough."

"You like that?" Slater said, putting his hands on his hips.

"It makes me think." He waved his arm, blushing. "Maybe you should, you know, show me who's boss."

"You mean you need some direction? A firm hand, that kind of thing?"

Ryan slowly nodded his head.

Furrowing his brow, Slater jutted his chin. "Have you been misbehaving?"

"Yes, sir," Ryan said. "I've been bad. Real bad."

"Show me your hands," Slater snapped.

He inhaled sharply and held out his palms, his eyes bright with anticipation. Slater stepped closer and grabbed his wrist, twisting it behind his back. Ryan yelped in surprise as he was spun around, even though it wasn't forceful enough to hurt. Slater grabbed his other wrist and pinned them together. With his other hand, he grabbed Ryan's throat and pulled him close.

Leaning into his ear, Slater growled, "Your behavior has consequences."

"Please," Ryan said. "I didn't mean it. Show me mercy."

Slater swung him around to the futon and pushed him face-down, then straddled him, grinding his swelling woody into him.

"I have no reason to be merciful. Not until you've earned it." Before he let go of his wrists, he added, "Don't move."

Rising, he slid off his jeans, but left on the black T-shirt, and then grabbed a condom. Once he'd rolled it on, he worked his way into Ryan, moving slowly and keeping a tight grip on one of his wrists. Ryan groaned as Slater built up a rhythm, soon pounding him.

"Mercy," Ryan cried, and Slater came, straining into him.

After a moment, Slater climbed off, wrapping an arm around him and pulling him onto his back. Sitting up, he grabbed Ryan's throat in one hand, and Ryan reflexively grabbed his arm, but he didn't try to pull it away. Ryan was rock-hard, and Slater took him into his mouth, working him for the brief time it took him to climax.

Catching his breath, Slater stretched out and folded his arm over his eyes.

"That was freaking amazing," Ryan said, still panting.

Slater lifted his arm, and turned to him, and said softly in his ear, "You're forgiven."

With a shuddering breath, Ryan moved closer, wrapping an arm around his belly, and squeezed him tightly.

Once the guy was breathing in the regular rhythm of sleep, Slater extracted himself and pulled off the sweaty black T-shirt, then went to the kitchen to slam his ration of bourbon. He drank from the bottle, suppressing a cough from the tickle of the intense fumes, and returned to bed content with the burgeoning fire in his belly.

TWELVE

RYAN WAS UP AND dressed, sitting on the sofa with his laptop, by the time Slater woke.

"I have some other stuff to do today," Ryan said, rising and folding his computer.

"OK." Slater watched him sling on his day pack. Whatever he was hiding, he was really bad at it.

"I'm going to the central library to do some document research."

"Where did we leave things with Norma López?"

"She has my number," Ryan said. "What are you working on today?"

"The fracking company. Let me know when you hear from Kawamura."

Ryan nodded and moved toward the door.

"Do you need help moving the Polara?"

"Wedging it in there freaks me out, but I think I can handle backing it into the alley."

Slater heard him lock the door behind him as he left. It was great to be rid of him for the day—almost like he had his life back.

Climbing into bed again, he wanted to doze some more, but first he looked up McInnes Shale Oil. A business listing said that the company did fracking chemistry, not the actual drilling. He searched for "fracking chemistry" and read about the process. It sounded nasty, pumping a toxic cocktail of chemicals into the ground so that they could extract more hydrocarbons. Detractors claimed it would poison the groundwater for centuries.

McInnes's office was in Long Beach, but before he went there, he wanted to swing by that bookstore. It was a dick move to double-check someone else's work, but that only applied when it was someone he trusted, and that didn't include Ryan. The guy had been acting squirrely, lying about something. A ride to La Mirada would reveal how much of what he'd told him was the truth. He found the address for Armada Books, and put it in his navigation app, then rolled out of bed to get dressed.

He threw the SECURITY shirt on the laundry

pile in his closet, grinning at the memory of Ryan's reaction to it. That guy was full of surprises—and he had his secrets. Who was the authority figure Slater stood in for, the one he needed to show him mercy?

Once he was dressed, he trotted down to the garage and backed the Thunderbird into the alley, and waited for the door to roll down, then headed for the freeway. It was overcast, he realized. He should probably check the weather. It hardly ever rained, but October was the start of the season.

The bookstore was a few minutes off the 5 in one of those outdoor malls that were ubiquitous around the metropolis, with shops surrounding a sea of parking. He couldn't tell whether the big blue letters over the door that spelled out ARMADA BOOKS had been rearranged, but each letter was a separately installed piece of hardware, so it was possible—and didn't contradict Im Hae's story.

When he stepped inside, the place was devoid of customers. A lone clerk stood behind the desk near the door. In his early twenties, he had Latin coloring, and sleek black hair, and muscular arms.

"Can I help you?" he said, as Slater approached.

"I was in here a while back. A woman named Norma helped me find some books. Is she around?"

"Norma helped you?" he said, raising his eyebrows. "That's surprising."

"Why is that?"

"She's not really a book person. I'm sure she has a vague idea of what they're used for, but I can't imagine she'd be able to point you to a specific one. Norma just ran the till—until she got fired."

Slater frowned. "Are you sure it's the same woman? Norma López. Long dark hair, a little curvy, wears miniskirts."

"That's the one."

"Why did she get canned?"

The guy leaned in and lowered his voice, even though there was no one around to overhear. "I heard drugs were involved."

"What was she on?" Slater said.

"I'm not sure. She never seemed especially sedated or speedy." He slid his hands into the pockets of his chinos, revealing the pleasing contour of his pecs beneath his shirt. "She works over at the mall in Cerritos now. At one of the kiosks. I think it's called Cell Phone Bros."

Slater nodded. "So do you work out?"

He laughed, revealing a set of even white teeth. "That sounds like a pickup line."

"Is it working?"

His eyes narrowed. "It depends on what you had in mind."

Slater jutted his chin toward the doorway behind him. "I could smoke you in the back room."

"That is so trashy," he said, and frowned. "Let

me see if there are any customers."

He walked around the end of the bookshelves, then went to the front door and flipped the sign from OPEN to CLOSED, and twisted the bolt to lock it. Following him into the back room, Slater had to grin. Despite his indignant proclamation, the guy was down with trashy.

It was a confined space, with a desk at one end, and stacks of books and cardboard boxes piled haphazardly on industrial shelves along both sides. Closing the door behind them, the clerk turned to face him. Slater leaned in, mouthing his neck, and his jaw, and his ear, then met his mouth. He shoved the guy back against the shelves and reached for his belt, unbuckling it and pushing his trousers down to reveal his already engorged cock.

Kneeling in front of him, Slater took him into his mouth, and grasped his thighs, and worked him until he came. When he got there, the guy yelped and put a hand on Slater's head to stop him.

Rising again, Slater met his mouth, warm and taut and insistent. The guy groped his crotch, and then unbuttoned his jeans and pulled out his woody, deftly stroking it. Slater put a hand on the back of his neck and leaned in to breathe the heady scent of his hair. It only took a minute for him to climax.

Afterward, he let his weight sink into the guy

for a moment, breathing hard and feeling the warmth of his body. When he pulled away, the guy zipped up his chinos and buckled his belt, then adjusted his hair with his fingers.

"Well, that doesn't usually happen right after I open the shop."

"That surprises me," Slater said. "You're extremely hot."

The clerk scoffed at that, and grinned, then opened the door and went to the front entrance, flipping the sign over and twisting the bolt open. Slater followed him toward the door.

"So what book were you looking for today?" he said.

Slater frowned. "I don't need any books."

He walked out and strode over to his car. Once he was behind the wheel, he pulled up directions on his phone for that mall in Cerritos. He knew the place, but not how to get there from here. It was just a few minutes' drive.

This was a bigger complex, he saw, cruising into the surface lot. Part of it was outdoors, and there was a traditional indoor section. Slater parked and went inside, and walked nearly the length of the mall to find Cell Phone Bros, a little stand in the middle of the space, with racks of phone cases and lanyards and earphones.

The only person working the kiosk didn't fit Norma's description. She was a woman, based on the contours of the torso, he decided, once he got closer. Around thirty, androgynous and built wiry, with a buzzed haircut, she was perched on a stool at one side of the display, seemingly unconcerned about the inventory getting jacked, ignoring it in favor of her phone screen. Any lingering question about gender evaporated when Slater got a look at the front of the clerk's T-shirt, emblazoned with clear guidance: IT'S HE-HIM-HIS. As Slater approached, the guy looked up at him with dead eyes.

"Is Norma here today?" Slater said.

He raised his eyebrows. "Does it look like Norma's here today?"

Slater put his hands on his hips. "You can spare me the attitude, son. When does she come in?"

He grinned. "Probably tomorrow. There's only one of us on at a time, and I'm not working then. Who's asking?"

"You're scheduled to be here the rest of the day?"

He looked up at the ceiling and raised a languid palm. "God willing."

"Are you on tranquilizers or something?" Slater demanded.

"Screw you, you burnout," he snapped. "Norma's the supplier, not me. If you need your fix, you'll have to find her yourself, or look somewhere else."

"Does she actually deal from here?"

"You need to leave," he said, raising his voice. "Otherwise I'm calling security."

"Predictable, from a gunsel," Slater said, jutting his chin, and then turned on his heel.

Walking back to his car, he wasn't sure whether that clerk was a bona fide lowlife or just a dick. Some of those plastic-junk shills were connected to the syndicates. More significant, he'd implied that Norma was a drug dealer. Ryan hadn't picked up on that—Slater should have talked to her himself.

His next stop was McInnes Shale Oil, and once he was behind the wheel, he pulled out his phone to find the address in his navigation app. At least it was in this part of town. Once he'd found his way out of the mall, he took the ramp onto the 605.

The place wasn't really in Long Beach, he realized, as he drove into the area. It was an industrial zone near the Long Beach airport. The neighborhoods like this east of downtown were for logistics, but this one was about oil. There were petroleum deposits all over the basin, sometimes even oozing out at the surface, and he knew there were lots of active wells, but the machinations of the business weren't usually so visible. The derricks were long gone, but storage tanks perched on several of the hilltops, and he drove past a gnarly clot of angular surface pipelines and valves.

McInnes's office was in a row of low window-less buildings interspersed with heavily fortified yards, coils of razor wire looping along the fence tops, all of it partly obscured by the acacias lining the street. Slater parked out front and looked the place over. Squat and whitewashed, the building had a truck gate at one side that was padlocked shut, and a door facing the street with a small sign mounted next to it marked MCINNES.

When he tried the door, it was unlocked, and he stepped inside. There was no receptionist, no front office, just a room with half a dozen desks and computers, and a counter along the side with an array of electronic equipment. It looked like a technical workspace, but not like a laboratory—they weren't working with chemicals in here.

Three guys sat at the desks, all of them wear-ing white dress shirts, and all of them Anglo. The man at the back was thick and had graying hair. Across from him was a younger guy, in his thir-ties and skinny, with a broken nose. Closer to the door was a huge man, also parked at a desk. More than overweight, he was muscular, and had unctuous acne-scarred skin. All of them looked up in surprise. They clearly didn't get many unex-pected visitors.

The thick one at the back said, "What can I do for you, son?"

Slater stepped closer. "Is one of you McInnes?"

"Who's asking?" he said evenly.

Something was wrong with this place, he realized. He couldn't pin it down, exactly, but he could feel it at the back of his neck. Almost like they were gangsters. Maybe this was a front company for a syndicate. But that didn't quite fit either.

"The name is John Slade," he said.

"What's your business here?"

"Tell me about Marvel-Anne."

He threw his head back and guffawed. "Now, why would I do that?"

"Why wouldn't you do that?" Slater demanded. "What kind of bunco are you running here?"

The big guy leisurely got up and rolled his neck to one side, a wry grin on his face, then took a step toward him.

"I'm thinking you're not McInnes," Slater said. "You're the muscle. They wouldn't put your name on the door."

"They call me Mr. K."

"Stay where you are, big guy. We're just having a conversation. Don't be crowding me."

"You should run along," Mr. K. said, and casually squeezed his fist with his other hand, audibly cracking the knuckles.

"Does the *k* stand for knucklehead?" Slater demanded. "Just tell me what I want to know, and nobody needs to get hurt."

"*Knucklehead* starts with an *n*, smart guy. And you're the only one who's going to get hurt."

With no warning, the big guy threw a punch, a heavy right, and even though he wasn't standing that close to Slater, it was close enough to connect. Slater managed to loosen up when he saw it coming, and shift slightly to lessen the impact. It caught him on his left eye and spun his head sideways.

Snapping back, Slater went low, into a crouch, and hit the guy with a gut punch. His abs were solid boards, and the blow had little effect. As he retreated, Mr. K. lunged and grabbed Slater under the arms, around the chest, and started to lift and squeeze, a suffocating bear hug. It was such a stupid move—it left his junk exposed. Using all the force he could muster without being able to take a breath, Slater swung up and kneed him in the crotch.

The guy groaned and let go of him, then doubled over. As Slater backed away, panting to catch his breath, Mr. K. tried to straighten up. His face was red, and he lurched toward him, but Slater was already at the door, then outside, trotting toward the street. Glancing back, he saw that the big guy wasn't following him. That was no surprise—he'd be dealing with a heap of pain. A dick punch had the same impact on anyone with testes, no matter how much muscle you had.

As he climbed into his car, Slater rubbed his eye and looked at it in the rearview. It was really going to piss him off if it bruised. Taking a breath to dispel the adrenaline, he started the engine and pulled into the street.

Those other two were accustomed to fisticuffs—they hadn't even raised an eyebrow when Mr. K. started the dustup. Oil industry people were rough, he knew that, but he hadn't expected full-blown lowlifes. More than anything, Mr. K. looked like an enforcer. What had Slater walked into?

He was accelerating up the freeway ramp when his phone rang. It was Ryan.

"Ibáñez," he said as he picked up.

"I heard back from Kawamura. He admitted that he's in Venice. Just taking a break, he said, and hanging out at the beach."

"Did you ask him where he's staying?"

"A short-term rental, he said. Once he knew he was busted, he said we could get together at some point."

"If he's on vacation," Slater said, "he could bug out at any minute. I'll go talk to him today."

"Shouldn't I be there too?"

"You two have a lot of history. Let me interview him first."

"We didn't actually make a plan about where to meet."

"Let me get over to Venice, and then you can phone him back. Tell him you hired me to look for Marvel-Anne, so I need a few minutes of his time. On short notice it'll be harder for him to say no."

"I wonder if there's any point?" Ryan said. "He's going to tell you the same thing—he doesn't know anything about Marvel-Anne."

"If he pushes back, you tell him that it's starting to look like he's hiding something," Slater said. "I'm on my way there. I'll call you in a few minutes."

He was already on the 405, and he stayed with it, headed west instead of back downtown. Venice wasn't a big neighborhood, and the south side was more gentrified, with more vacation rentals, so he headed there. He exited the freeway and drove west, and found a meter space on the boulevard a few blocks from the beach. Once he'd killed the engine, he sent Ryan a text:

Call him now.

A few minutes later his phone rang.

"Kawamura wants to meet at a diner," Ryan said, and gave him the name of the place. "He's not happy about being interviewed."

"He's smart not to refuse. That would only make me dig deeper."

Slater ended the call and looked up the diner

on his phone. It was nearby, a little closer to the beach. Climbing out of the Thunderbird, he walked a few blocks, and soon found the place. It was on a corner and had lots of glass facing both streets—exactly the kind of place a security-oriented guy would pick for a meeting with a stranger.

A few people sat at the tables, but none of them were Kawamura. Slater took a stool at the counter. A tired-looking waitress came over and raised her eyebrows.

"Coffee," he told her.

She set the steaming cup in front of him just as Kawamura walked in. The guy was tall, and wearing a tan suit over a white dress shirt. That seemed like an odd outfit for a beach vacation. As Kawamura paused to scan the room, Slater spotted the telltale bulge under his suit jacket. He wore his weapon like Max did, in a holster under his arm.

Slater waved, and Kawamura scowled in annoyance as he walked over, briefly producing a handkerchief to mop his brow. He was sweating, even though it wasn't warm out—he'd walked here. Parking was always a pain in Venice, so he'd likely picked this place because it was near his rental.

"Ryan hired you?" Kawamura said, sliding onto the stool beside him.

"That's right." Slater handed him his business card.

He studied the card briefly before tucking it into his jacket. "Why?"

"Like he told you, he's looking for his business partner. He said you don't seem at all concerned that Marvel-Anne is missing."

"Marvel-Anne is an adult." He eyed Slater sidelong. "She can take care of herself."

The waitress stepped over. "What'll it be, hon?"

"Just a coffee," Kawamura said.

"When is the last time you saw Marvel-Anne?"

"The day I left her and Ryan at the bed-and-breakfast on the Washougal River."

"Did she say anything about her plans?" Slater said. "Some trip she was going to take without Ryan?"

"Not a word. I'm not that close to either of them."

The waitress set a mug in front of him, and Kawamura flashed a smile and thanked her. This guy was American, Slater thought, and from the way he spoke he knew he was a native speaker, but he still had the muscle memory of Japanese manners.

"Where do you think she'd go?"

"I have no idea," he said firmly. "Why does Ryan think she's in Los Angeles?"

"She contacted a couple of people here, and sold some equipment."

Kawamura's brow furrowed. "I see. I'm sorry I can't assist you in Ryan's quest. I can't tell you anything more about Marvel-Anne than what Ryan already knows."

That was all he was going to get, Slater realized. True to his podcast persona, Kawamura was not a chatty guy.

"You know martial arts, I take it," Slater said.

Kawamura eyed him. "Why do you say that?"

"People with those skills are often very calm, like you are right now. I suppose it's because you know you can defend yourself."

A smile played on his lips. "I have some skills. I trained in karate and iaido."

"Is that the one with the swords?" Slater said. "Yikes."

He was glad he'd asked. People who were advanced at martial arts—the masters and the teachers—usually believed that they had minimal skill. Someone had once explained it to him as, "The more you learn, the more you realize how much you don't know." Kawamura's confidence in himself meant that he likely wasn't all that advanced. Iaido had always felt more like performance art than self-defense anyway—in this day and age you couldn't actually cut people for practice.

"So you could probably put me in the hospital

with one punch," Slater said.

Kawamura tapped a finger under his own eye. "It looks like someone already tried to do that to you."

"Damn it," Slater muttered, and rubbed his eye. It must be starting to bruise. "So why didn't you tell Ryan you were in town?"

"Because he's spinning his wheels. Looking for someone who doesn't want to be found."

"Why doesn't she want to talk to him?"

"That's not my business," Kawamura said.

He twisted sideways on the stool, toward Slater, and let his jacket fall open. The butt of his weapon was clearly visible. It looked like a basic Glock. Was he trying to threaten him?

"Tell Ryan that maybe it's better if he doesn't find her."

"Why not?" Slater demanded.

"Ryan isn't telling you everything."

"That's good to know. What is it that he isn't telling me?"

"Again, it's not my business."

Slater dropped his chin and pointedly eyed his weapon, then looked up and met his gaze. "I guess I'm not going to argue with you."

Kawamura stood up and dug into his front pocket.

"Forget about it," Slater said. "I'll buy your coffee."

"Thank you," he said, eyeing him for a moment, and then walked toward the door.

As soon as he was past the windows and out of sight, Slater got up and dug out his wad of cash, and peeled off a sawbuck. The waitress came over and eyed the untouched coffees.

"Will that cover it?" Slater said, dropping the bill on the counter.

She nodded as she reached for it. "Sure thing, hon."

Hustling out to the street, Slater looked in the direction Kawamura had gone. The guy walked fast—he could see the tan suit half a block ahead. Was he savvy enough to be wary of a tail?

As Slater followed him, though, hustling to catch up, Kawamura didn't look back. A minute later he turned into a side street, and as Slater reached the corner, he saw him stop in front of a gate in a high redwood fence, and open it with a key, and then disappear inside.

Slowing his pace, Slater walked up to the house. It was new construction, built like a fortress to fill most of the lot, its high fences dwarfing the open front yards of the older prewar bungalows on the block. There were so many of these now, it made the neighborhood feel balkanized, walled off, like the fortified compounds that rich people built in the Third World.

At least there were no cameras, Slater saw,

scanning the fence and the glassy house towering above. Even though there were homeless encampments within blocks of here, it made sense—short-term rental guests didn't want to feel like they were being spied on.

Farther along, the garage door was only halfway down, with a huge Mercedes SUV parked inside that was too long to fit in the space. The grill and the front quarter panels were exposed, and it had a Cali license plate. A spattering of water droplets dotted the hood, but the street and the sidewalk were dry. It must have drizzled earlier. Slater glanced around to make sure he wasn't being observed, then ducked under the garage door.

The Mercedes had a little rental-car barcode sticker in the driver's window. That meant Kawamura hadn't come to town with his own wheels. At the rear end of the vehicle was the door into the house. Slater stepped over to it and gingerly tried the handle. It was unlocked. That was an idiot move for a security guy—the junkies could easily jack his stuff, and half the homeless population of Venice could move in here with him.

Opening the door a crack, he listened for a moment, but heard no sound. Slater opened it farther and stepped inside. It was a foyer, with the front door, and a coat rack, and a flight of stairs leading up. It made sense that the ground floor of the house was just this and the garage, as there were at least two more floors overhead.

Next to the front door was a panel for the alarm. It was a basic consumer system, and the screen flashed DISABLED. That meant more than just disarmed, or switched off—whoever owned the house had quit paying the security company. That might be useful. Eyeing the deadbolt on the front door, he saw that it was a standard model too.

On the bench next to the door was a black box, a piece of electronic hardware. It looked a little like the audio equipment Marvel-Anne had sold. Had they both mopped gear from Ryan's project? Pulling out his phone, he squatted and focused the camera on the label that bore the name of the manufacturer and the model number, and took a photo.

Treading back to the garage, Slater gently closed the door behind him and walked the length of the Mercedes, ducking under the big door to emerge on the street. A woman was walking by, on the opposite side, and she glanced over at him. But this was a rental house—she wouldn't know he wasn't supposed to be here.

Flashing her a smile, he strode back toward the boulevard and found the Thunderbird.

THIRTEEN

ONCE HE'D PARKED IN the lot across from his office, Slater eyed the new parking attendant in the wide-brimmed hat, and waved, eliciting a wary wave in response. There was a *lonchera* parked at the end of the block, he saw, and he went down and bought a couple of tacos, with jackfruit and beans and lettuce, and ate them nearby, over the gutter.

Up in his office, he flicked on the lights and eyed Rey Pascual.

"Just you and me, man," he said, and then checked Max's office before he went into his own, where he got comfortable at his desk. Online he read more about fracking chemistry. Most of it was mundane, but he found it interesting that they used nitroglycerin in the work.

His head was starting to ache as he stared at the screen, and his ribs ached where that gorilla had manhandled him. Pulling open his desk drawer, he found a bottle of ibuprofen, and shook out a couple, then got up and walked down the hall to the restroom for water. Popping the tablets, he cupped his hands under the tap to drink, then ran a wet hand through his hair. In the mirror he could see the telltale red half-moon under his eye. It was definitely going to bruise.

"Damn it," he muttered.

On the way back to the office, he found Max walking around from the elevator, wearing his gray suit, keys in hand.

"Whoa," Max said. "What's with the shiner?"

"I blame the oil industry," Slater said, and followed him inside, dropping into the chair in front of Max's desk. As Max got settled, he told him about the run-in with Mr. K., and about meeting Kawamura.

"It's a little odd that he's packing a weapon," Max said. "If he's from out of state, there's no reciprocity in Cali for a concealed carry permit."

"I know they worked on the podcast in northern California. Humboldt and Trinity and Shasta."

"Where the bigfeet live," Max said. "That makes sense—it's way easier to get a weapons permit in the rural counties."

"Are you still working that window-shade case?"

"I'm tracking the alleged cheater, but she's slippery. I just came in to make some notes."

"I hate those jobs."

"You're good at them, though," Max said. "You wrapped it up for that Armenian guy in a single night with the photos you got. I was thinking today that I wish I'd had that kind of luck on this case."

"Do you know anything about nitroglycerin?"

Max shifted in his chair. "Old-timers call it safecracker soup, or just nitro. I know you don't want to mess with that stuff. If you drop it, or even jostle it, *kablooey.*"

"How much of it do they use to open a safe?"

"The guy who told me about it said he used an eyedropper," Max said. "So maybe half an ounce? He said it would blow the door right off. The problem was that it would burn up any paper inside, so it was only useful to get to jewelry or gold."

"Excellent," Slater said, and got up.

"I'm glad you didn't ask me where to get some. Do you have a safe you need to open?"

Slater chuckled. "Just gathering intel."

Back at his own desk, he read more about nitroglycerin, and its role in fracking, and how dangerous it was. California had banned transporting it in the 1860s when a crate of it blew up and killed a warehouse full of people.

Finally he locked his computer, and called good-bye to Max, and went down to his car.

In the Arts District, just a few minutes' drive, he knew there was a cannabis lab supply store. It wasn't a pot shop, so it didn't have armed security and bank-vault entry doors, just an airy storefront with a sleek distressed-wood facade. Slater found a street space to park and then walked inside.

Next to the front desk was a potted Japanese maple with vibrant green leaves, and Slater paused to admire it. It was healthy and well tended. It would be content in this indirect lighting—even the red-leaved cultivars needed low light.

The clerk, a guy in his early thirties, stepped over. He had a waxed mustache and a beard that was two shades darker than the hair on his head. Slater used to think some Anglo guys dyed their hair, but he'd seen so many of them with that two-tone effect, it had to be natural. The mustache looked fussy, but he was essentially fuckable.

Slater brushed his fingers under the leaves of the maple. "This is clever."

Two-tone grinned. "You can tell it's not really marijuana."

"I get what you're doing. The leaves are similar. Is it the Seiryu cultivar?"

"That's not what it's called. It's a Japanese maple."

"Well—that explains everything. I take it you're not the one who tends to it."

"What can I help you with?"

"I need a clear glass bottle with a rubber stopper," Slater said, and held his palms a few inches apart. "About this big."

"Is it for distillation?"

"Just for storage."

"Does it need to be tempered?"

Slater frowned. "What does that mean?"

"If you're putting hot extracts in it, or heating them in the container, tempered glass won't crack from heat stress."

"I'm not a doper. I just need a bottle that looks like lab equipment."

"Cannabis is a legitimate industry," the guy said, his brow furrowing.

"It's also dope. Which is probably why you have a Japanese maple out front, not an actual cannabis plant."

Two-tone scowled, but said, "This way," and led him deeper into the shop, to a shelf with an array of glassware. "These are the tempered flasks. Capacity is eight or sixteen ounces."

Slater looked over the options. The shape was right, with the wide base tapering to a narrow neck.

"The smaller one."

"I can sell you a stopper with holes in it, or solid."

"The solid one makes a tight seal?" Slater said.

"That's the idea."

"Let's do that."

The clerk carried the flask and a black stopper to the desk at the front.

"Thirty-two for the pair," he said, keying it into the register.

Slater pulled out his wad of cash and counted out the bills. "That's definitely a pot-industry price."

"If you're not in the industry," the clerk said, tucking the flask into a paper sack, "what are you using them for?"

"Nitro," Slater said, meeting his gaze. He took the bag and walked out to his car.

There were some discount places that sold perfume near his office in the Fashion District, he knew, and he turned onto a likely street, scanning the storefronts as he cruised. On the right side a place had MONDO PERFUME in big red letters above the door—that would do it.

He found an open parking meter and pulled in, then walked back to the shop. When he stepped inside, the clerk looked up and greeted him in Spanish. She was in her fifties, with long black hair, and wore a billowy fuchsia blouse.

"I need your cheapest perfume," Slater said, approaching her.

"A true romantic," she said, and stepped out from the counter. Walking closer to the door, she pointed out a low shelf. "These are all under thirty."

"I need a lot of it," Slater said.

She stifled a sigh and reached for a little bottle. "This one is sixteen bucks for two ounces. Would you like to try it?"

"No need. I'll take three of those," he said, and dug in his pants for his cash.

"Three different girlfriends?" she said, stepping back to the counter.

Slater frowned as he handed her a C-note. "I only date guys."

"Well, they're all going to appreciate this one." She tucked the bottles into a bag and handed it to him, then made change.

When he got back to the office, Max was gone. Slater went down the hall to the men's room with the flask and the perfume. When he opened the first little bottle, it struck his nose with a musky, flowery odor and a distinct chemical undertone. He dumped it into the flask, which made the smell even stronger. This was potent stuff.

Slater screwed the cap tightly onto the empty bottle before he ditched it in the trash—no need to assault the janitor with that odor. Once he'd dumped the other bottles into the flask, he pressed in the rubber stopper, and held it up to the light. It looked suitably toxic: oily with a yellowish tint.

He spent a minute scrubbing his hands, using the soap, but he could still smell the stuff. Either it wasn't going to come off his fingers, or it was hanging in the air. Eventually he gave up and put the flask into its paper bag, then went down to his car.

Traffic was slowing down in the late afternoon, and it took longer to get to McInnes's office than it had earlier in the day. Eventually he pulled up to the curb in front and parked, then unbagged the flask and climbed out.

On the way to the door, Slater held the vessel out in front of him, upright in his palm, and paused for a moment to let the oily contents become still.

When he pulled open the door and stepped inside, the thick guy was at his desk near the back, and the skinny one with the broken nose was standing at the counter at the side of the room, but Mr. K. wasn't here. Both men turned to look as he entered.

"Just Frick and Frack?" Slater said. "Where's your gorilla?"

"He'll be back," the older guy said, and swiveled his chair to face him.

"That's too bad. I was looking forward to

giving him a tune-up."

The skinny guy scoffed. "Funny—from what I can see, you're the one who got the tune-up."

"I'm thinking he's the boss," Slater said, gesturing with his free hand to the guy at the desk. "You don't seem quite smart enough." He eyed the older man. "You're McInnes."

"What's in the bottle?" McInnes said.

"If you guys really are in the oilfield business, you've heard of this stuff. It's called nitro."

"Bullshit," the skinny guy said.

But McInnes's face clouded with concern. "Where did you get that?"

"It's not that hard to find. In my business it's called safecracker soup."

"You can't just walk around with that stuff," the skinny guy said intently. "It's not stable."

"So I'm told. But I made it here. Tell me about Marvel-Anne."

"I'm not going to tell you anything," the skinny guy said, his lip curling in disgust.

Slater held the bottle higher, careful not to jostle it. "From over here, I'll be able to avoid the blast, but you two won't."

"Are you crazy?" he demanded, and took a step toward him, waving his arms. "With that much nitro, you'll take down the whole building."

"Not one more fucking step," Slater growled.

"Settle down," McInnes said, a command

that the younger guy obeyed. He looked to Slater. "There's no need to be coarse. I can tell you about Marvel-Anne."

"First, Frick needs to sit."

The guy hesitated, but then moved toward the desk across from McInnes, and sat, twisting toward Slater and glaring at him.

"Marvel-Anne is a real nice gal," McInnes said, his tone calm, even affable. "Real good manners. She trained as a geologist. It's a great career for anyone who likes to be outdoors a lot."

"Is she working here?"

"She never worked with us, although we have mutual acquaintances in the industry. Marvel-Anne brokered a security deal for me."

"Meaning what?"

"We have our own security guards at our well sites. People like Mr. K. So that the flower-power morons and people like you can't interfere with the business. Marvel-Anne helped us acquire some weaponry."

"Like what, exactly?"

"Three assault rifles." He raised his eyebrows. "All permitted and registered and perfectly legal. Not that I'm obligated to explain my business to you."

"When are you meeting her again?"

"The deal is done," McInnes said, and gestured expansively. "We got the equipment, and she got paid. I'm not planning to see her again."

Slater pulled out his phone. "Give me her contact number."

McInnes picked up the cell phone on his desk and recited it. Slater didn't have to make note of it—the number was the one Ryan had given him for Marvel-Anne.

"I'm not sure that really is nitro," the skinny guy said. "How did you get it here? Why didn't it blow up your car?"

"We don't need to press the matter," McInnes said. "The gentleman was just leaving."

"He's no gentleman. He's a goddamn wetback."

"I was actually born here," Slater said, affecting a nonchalant tone. "I didn't have to cross any rivers. But I think your implication is that you have more right to be here than me because of your inbred pasty white skin."

"Where would a wetback get nitro?" he said. "I can't figure it out."

"You know, the only mistake I made was buying a tempered flask," Slater said. "I didn't even consider that it might not break very easily. Let's hope this works."

Slater grasped the neck of the flask and hurled it overhand, like a fastball, with as much force as he could muster. It struck the concrete floor between their desks and shattered with a loud *pop*, spraying liquid in a wide arc. The skinny guy emitted a high-pitched scream.

"It smells like perfume," McInnes said, half out of his chair now and glaring at him. "You said it was nitro."

"I'll add you two to my sucker list," Slater said, and walked out. What a pair of idiots.

As he approached his car, he heard footsteps behind him, and spun around. It was the skinny guy with the broken nose, rage in his eyes, fists balled. He took a swing, and Slater easily dodged it, responding with a solid right hook to the jaw. As the guy's head spun, Slater struck with a gut punch. The guy collapsed, his body curling in around his belly.

"Why do you make me do this to you?" Slater shouted, and kicked him in the ribs. The guy moaned and rolled onto his side. "You racist fuck." He kicked him in the kidney, and then forced himself to step back, surveying his crumpled form. This was a textbook loudmouth—unlimited confidence and zero brawling chops. Slater took a deep breath, willing himself to let go of it. He looked around. No witnesses—McInnes hadn't even bothered to come outside.

"Next time, send Mr. K.," he shouted at him, then walked over to the Thunderbird.

———◦———

DAYLIGHT WAS FADING AS Slater parked in the surface lot behind Andy's building. He walked around to the entrance and went upstairs. When Andy answered the door, he was wearing his usual tank top and boxers.

"Why didn't you … text?" Andy said.

Slater followed him inside. "I was driving."

"You wanted to … catch me with Kyle."

"Stop talking about him."

Andy turned to face him, then peered at his eye. "That looks painful."

"Not really. I didn't get out of the way in time."

"I'd hate to see what the … other guy looks like."

"I stepped away from that fight," Slater said. "He was three times my size."

Andy leaned against his computer desk. "So are you here for business or pleasure?"

"I need you to dig into someone for me. Anything you can get that's not mundane."

"What details do you have?"

"A cell number, and a photo, maybe an address. His name is Kawamura. I'll send you what I've got."

Andy watched as Slater pulled out his phone and tapped at it. "Do you have time to mess around?"

"Always," Slater said, glancing up at him.

"Unless you're too wiped out from boning twinky Kyle."

"I thought you didn't want to talk about him."

Andy moved to the bed and sat on the edge. Slater knelt in front of him, pushing his knees apart. He ran his hands over his back, and kissed his bare shoulder, and breathed in the heady scent of his armpits.

"Are you wearing cologne?" Andy said.

"I was handling some earlier. It's hard to wash off."

"I won't ask."

Andy ran a hand into his hair as Slater mouthed his neck. Slater's phone buzzed in the pocket of his jeans, and he reached down for a moment to squeeze it into silence. It rang again a moment later, and he pulled away.

"Don't answer it," Andy said.

When he sat back on his heels, and pulled it out to check, he saw that it was Ryan. "I have to," he said. Picking up, he answered sharply, "Ibáñez."

"I need you to hear something," Ryan said. "Where are you?"

"You sound upset."

"I am upset. Can I come to your office?"

"If it's urgent, I can be there in a few minutes."

Andy eyed him as he ended the call. "You're ditching me."

"It's work."

"You're wasting this," Andy said, and stood up, his woody tenting his boxers.

He put his hands behind Slater's head and pulled him into his crotch. Slater took a playful bite at his dick through the fabric. That activated Andy's startle reflex—he jumped like he'd had an electric shock.

Rising to his feet, he kissed Andy again, then met his gaze. "We'll get to that another time. Later, beautiful."

FOURTEEN

WHEN SLATER GOT UP to his office, there was no sign of Max. He sat at his desk and checked the tracker on the Polara. It was just a few blocks from here, and getting closer. The circle on the map representing its estimated location hopped from point to point on its way up the street.

Before that, it had been parked near the central library, and then at the Natural History Museum again. Maybe Ryan was at some other place near there, some library or archive, and was just using the museum's parking lot. He tried to remember what else was around it, but all he could come up with was another museum, and government offices, and the rose garden.

When Ryan knocked at the office door, Slater

got up to unlock it for him.

"Are you wearing cologne?" Ryan said, following him back to his desk.

"I was handling some earlier."

"What happened to your eye?"

"That oil company has aggressive goons." Slater waved impatiently as he sat in his chair. "What's so urgent?"

"This voice mail," Ryan said, and set his phone on the desktop, leaning over it to start the playback. It was a man's voice, gruff and muffled.

"If you really want to find your girlfriend," he said, "she'll be at 1432½ Roseview Walk until eight."

"That's it?" Slater said. "Who the hell is that?"

"I have no clue. The caller ID said 'unknown.' But it has to be about Marvel-Anne."

"Who knows that you're looking for her?"

Ryan sat back and frowned in thought. "You, and Kawamura, and Im Hae. Also the guy who works at Armada Books, and Norma López."

"This feels really fishy."

"Because he didn't leave his name?"

"The caller wasn't any of those people, was it?"

"I don't think so. What about the television producer you met, and Marvel-Anne's ex-boyfriend, the photographer?"

"They'd call me, not you." Slater reclined in his chair. "Kawamura has no reason to hide his identity. Im Hae isn't a lowlife. The bookstore guy doesn't even know Marvel-Anne, so he wouldn't care if she lived or died. That leaves Norma López. When you met her, did she seem like a lowlife?"

"I'm not sure how to determine that. She works in retail. It didn't feel like a criminal enterprise. But she was a little cagey when she talked about Marvel-Anne." Ryan gestured impatiently. "Look, it's close to eight. Should we go?"

"I'll go," Slater said, and typed the address into his phone. "It's not far. I'll call you after."

Ryan nodded. "If you think that's best."

Slater watched him for a moment. It was suspicious that he didn't protest. Surely he was curious enough to want to go with him, or at least to press Slater on what he planned to do.

"Give me a second," Slater said, and turned to his computer. He typed a quick email to Max:

> If I disappear, I'm headed to a meeting at eight p.m. at 1432½ Roseview Walk. It smells like a setup. Ryan, the Sasquatch guy, has more details.

He set it to delay sending until tomorrow morning. That way, if he didn't have trouble tonight, he could delete it before it went out. Locking the computer with a keystroke, Slater rose and waved Ryan out the front door, pausing to twist his key in the deadbolt. In the elevator down to the street, he eyed Ryan again.

"You have absolutely no idea who might have left that message? Not even a guess?"

Ryan shrugged. "It sounded like an old man."

"You haven't asked anyone else about Marvel-Anne?"

"Just the people you know about."

As they crossed the street to the parking lot, it started to rain. Slater climbed into the Thunderbird and watched Ryan get into the nearby Polara, the view distorted through the wet spatter on the windshield. He flicked on the wipers and his headlights and pulled into the traffic, then headed for the freeway.

Roseview Walk. A "Walk" usually meant a gated pedestrian-only path, built in to some of the twentieth-century planned communities, but from where it appeared on the map, it was in a commercial district in Cypress Park. A few minutes later, on an industrial boulevard near the tracks, he pulled up at the end of the street.

It looked like an alley, and he could see it was gated at the far end of the block. So the "Walk" part was accurate in that respect—he could drive into it, but not through it. But "Roseview" was purely aspirational—no rosebush or any other greenery grew anywhere near here.

Driving to the next corner, Slater parked and walked back to the alley. Even though it wasn't raining hard enough to make him hustle, he strode at a brisk pace. A lone vehicle rolled by on the boulevard, but the sidewalk was deserted at this hour. Turning into the alley, he saw that it was poorly lit, but at least someone was keeping it clear of trash.

The alley was lined with fenced parking spaces and the back entrances to the businesses on the main street. Some were marked with company names—a bakery, a restaurant supplier, an electrician. No one was around, it seemed, and the gates were all closed. Most of them had street numbers posted, and he found the one cited in the voice mail, hand-drawn in faded paint on a steel door. Slater looked over the building. It was an otherwise unmarked commercial structure, with no fence or parking spaces, the back exit opening directly onto the alley.

The door was ajar, he saw, and he pulled it open, and stepped inside. It was dark, but he could feel carpeting under his feet. Slater ran a hand through his hair to dispel the raindrops, then saw the switch on the wall, and clicked on the room lights.

He was in a small office. A set of shelves lined the back wall, stacked with folders and bankers boxes, and in front of it was a desk. What made his heart pound was below that—a pair of sneaker-clad feet protruding from behind the desk.

Slater stepped over to look. Lying on his

back between the desk and the shelves was a guy dressed in dark-red jeans and a black shirt, his long brown hair splayed on the carpet around his head. One arm was twisted at a painful angle, maybe broken, and one side of his face was bruised and swollen. There was blood at his temple, but it wasn't pooling on the carpet.

Kneeling, Slater pressed two fingers to the guy's neck. His pulse was weak and thready, but he was still alive. He rose and looked around the space. There was a landline phone on the desk. He picked it up and dialed 911.

"You need to send an ambulance," Slater told the operator, and recited the address. "The guy is unconscious, but he still has a pulse."

"Are you rendering first aid?" the woman demanded.

"He's bleeding a little, but not enough to kill him."

"What happened there?"

"It looks like someone clobbered him. The door was open, and nobody else was here."

"I need you to stay on the line," she said. "What's your name?"

Slater hung up and then pulled out his handkerchief to wipe his prints off the receiver, and the number pad. Assessing the guy once more, he knew there was nothing he could do for him. There were no cameras here, he saw, briefly scanning the space. He went to the light switch and wiped it off, then pocketed his handkerchief and walked out, leaving the door ajar.

Slater jogged back to the boulevard, then slowed to a brisk walk. The neighborhood was quiet, but still, out here he might get noticed. Everything was wet, with puddles in the gutter, but the rain had let up.

There was no sign of a response yet, but it had only been a few minutes. He knew that the cops would get here first, and sure enough, as he reached his car, he heard the siren approaching.

Behind the wheel by the time the prowl car roared by, its flickering red and blue lights reflecting on the wet asphalt, Slater waited until it turned into the alley, then started the engine and nosed into the street.

He drove a few blocks and pulled over near a well-lit *tiendita*, then checked the tracking app on his phone for Conrad's location. The idiot was at his station. Slater dialed his cell, thankful that he picked up.

"I need to talk," Slater said.

"I don't have time for your bullshit right now," Conrad said. "I'm on my way home."

"I got into something. I might be in over my head." Slater listened, but there was no reply. "Can you meet me at that bar near my place?" he said finally.

Conrad sighed. "I'll head over there now."

Pulling back into the street, Slater navigated to the freeway and drove to Westlake. He found a place to park near the grubby little dive bar that he and Conrad used to go to sometimes. As he walked up on it, the reflected green and blue of its neon sign glistened on the wet pavement.

There were a few people in the booths, he saw as he stepped in—some raggedy old-time regulars here for the cheap booze, and a table of trendy college-age people here for the atmosphere. Conrad was wearing jeans and a yellow polo shirt, sitting on a barstool at the far end, away from the till and the service area. That was smart—they'd be less likely to be overheard. Slater walked over and sat beside him.

"Are you wearing cologne?" Conrad said, looking him over.

"No," Slater said flatly. "Why aren't you drinking?"

"I just sat down."

The bartender, a gruff-looking guy with black hair, came over and raised his eyebrows. Conrad ordered a small, and Slater asked for tonic water.

"That's not like you either," Conrad said.

Slater dug in his pocket and pulled out a twenty, folding it lengthwise and dropping it on the bar top.

Conrad frowned and tapped his own cheek,

under his eye. "What's this?"

"I walked into a door."

"More like you walked into a fist."

"Forget about that," Slater said, lowering his voice. "I found a guy. He was beat down and unconscious. In an office in Cypress Park."

"Did you call it in?"

"Of course I called it in. You people showed up right after I left."

"When did this happen?"

"Just now. A few minutes ago."

"Who was he?"

"I have no idea. I never saw the guy before. I think it was a setup to get me there, or to get my client there."

"Did you leave any prints?" Conrad said.

"No, but your techies are going to find my DNA."

"They won't check for DNA."

"If he dies, they will. He looked pretty messed up."

Slater paused as the bartender set down their drinks and took the twenty.

Conrad sipped his beer. "So you didn't stay to talk to the responding officers."

"Of course not," he hissed. "With my history, I'd be in the hoosegow right now."

"What took you there?"

"A lead on a case. I might know who sent me.

A lowlife named Norma López. She works retail at that mall in Cerritos, but I think she's also some kind of drug dealer."

Conrad dug in his hip pocket for his little notepad and pencil, and set it on the bar top to write down the details. Slater eyed the bartender, but he wasn't interested in what they were doing, standing at the other end of the bar.

"What's your connection to this woman?"

"I never met her," Slater said. "The information came through a third party."

He sighed. "You really should come in and make a statement."

"No way am I going to put myself in the middle of this. But I do want to know if you people are coming for me."

"I'll see what I can find out, and I'll get this name to whoever's investigating it."

"Can you do that without getting involved?"

"There's an anonymous reporting system for the public. I'll channel it through there." Conrad tucked his notepad away and took another mouthful of beer. "Don't call the hospitals or the coroner or anything like that," he said quietly. "Just let me dig."

"I owe you one."

Conrad scoffed and stepped off the stool. "You owe me many, Slater." As he walked toward the door, he muttered, "Many, many, many."

Watching him go, Slater admired his broad shoulders, his perfect butt. Such a beautiful man.

He sipped his tonic and pulled out his phone. Nothing from Ryan, which was really suspicious—why wasn't he curious about what he'd found? Running down Marvel-Anne was his whole purpose right now. The location tracker showed that after he'd left Slater's office, the Polara had moved a few blocks to the Historic Core. Slater texted him:

Where are you?

His reply came quickly:

Still downtown. Did you find Marvel-Anne?

He'd remembered that part, at least. Slater wrote back:

No. Meet me at this brewpub.

Once he'd found a listing for the place, on Sixth, near where the Polara was parked, he sent the address in another text.

He got up and gathered his change, leaving a couple of singles for the bartender, then headed out to the street.

FIFTEEN

<hr>

T WAS RAINING AGAIN as Slater pulled into a meter space near the brewpub. As he walked up on the place, Ryan was waiting outside, standing next to the wall under the overhang, out of the rain. When he caught sight of Slater, he smiled.

Slater balled his fists and strode up to him, and shoved him against the wall, pinning Ryan's clavicle under his forearm.

"Did you set me up?" Slater demanded.

Ryan's eyes grew wide. "What are you talking about?"

Stepping back, Slater slapped him, right and then left, a rapid kovac.

"Who was in that office?"

"What office?" Ryan shouted, and put a hand

to his cheek, glaring at him.

Slater grabbed his collar and moved closer. "Who left that voice mail?"

"I don't know. I thought we decided it was about Norma." He scowled. "Let go of me, and tell me what happened."

Slater studied his face. Indignation and fear. He was either a very good actor, or he was telling the truth. But nobody ever told the truth. Pressed against him like this, Slater realized he could feel wood at Ryan's crotch.

"You're into this." Slater ground his hips into him.

"I think it's a fear reaction. I'm scared of you right now."

Nearby, on the sidewalk, a guy holding an umbrella over his head paused and called, "Do you need help?"

"We're having a conversation here," Ryan said. "Move along."

"You know, you don't have to put up with that kind of treatment."

Slater pulled away from Ryan and eyed the guy. "Spread out."

He hesitated, his umbrella wavering.

"The man said beat it," Slater said, and jabbed a finger at him. "Do not make me come after you—I will fuck you up."

Finally the guy strode away.

He turned back to Ryan and took a breath. "I shouldn't be sleeping with you."

"You said it didn't change anything."

Leaning into him again, Slater kissed his neck, and then met his mouth. Ryan went with it for a minute, then pushed him off.

"There's a time and a place for everything."

"What are you talking about?" Slater demanded.

"This is neither the time nor the place for passion. It's a place to drink beer. Let's go inside."

As Slater pulled back, Ryan stepped away from the wall and adjusted his jacket, eyeing him from under a furrowed brow.

"You're a lot of man, Slater."

"And you're buying."

As they settled into a booth, Slater pushed the rain out of his hair with his hand. When the waitress stopped at their table, he ordered a draft pint and a burger.

Ryan frowned. "I thought you were vegan."

"Everything on the menu is plant-based," the waitress said.

"I guess I'll have the same."

As she stepped away, Slater said, "Give me your phone, and unlock it."

"Why?"

"My battery died. Come on." He waggled his fingers.

Ryan pulled it out, and thumb-typed the access code, then handed it across the table.

Slater sat back and tapped at the screen, installing the tracking app that he used, and typed in his credentials, then set it to run in hidden mode.

Watching him from across the table, Ryan's brow furrowed in concern. "Do you need to make a call or something?"

"Just checking my messages." He handed the phone back.

"Are you going to tell me what happened tonight, and why you have a black eye?"

"Norma López set me up. Or maybe you did."

"How can you think I'd do that to you?" Ryan demanded. "I'm the one who's paying you."

"I don't actually know what's going on. Not yet."

The waitress set down their beer, and Slater clinked his glass against Ryan's, and took a sip, then related what he'd found on Roseview Walk. He omitted the part about talking to Conrad. As he spoke, Ryan's face contorted with concern.

"Do you think he was going to die?" Ryan said.

"I'm not sure. He was pretty messed up. Whatever happens to him, you need to drop that whole angle. You're out of your depth."

"You think Norma left that message to lure me there? That she was using me?"

Slater shrugged. "Somebody was supposed to

take the fall for croaking that hippie."

"Are you sure you won't get caught up in it?"

"Not by choice. But if he dies, they'll definitely track me down."

Ryan sipped his beer. "If I'd gone myself, I would have waited for the police."

"And you'd be their prime suspect, sitting in a windowless little room right now, talking to two pushy cops."

"Why would Norma do that to me?"

"Norma doesn't know you, or give a damn about you. She has her own agenda." Holding his gaze, Slater said emphatically, "Do not talk to her again."

He waved a hand. "What did Kawamura say?"

"That you're not telling me everything."

Ryan frowned. "Is that why you roughed me up?"

"Nobody roughed you up," Slater said, and told him about meeting Kawamura, and following him back to his rental. "I saw some electronic equipment there." He pulled out his phone and found the photo he'd taken, then handed it across. "Do you know what that is?"

"I thought your phone battery died," he said, his brow furrowing.

"Not quite. I was afraid it would crash in the middle of my messages."

"It's a field mixer," Ryan said, studying the

image. He handed the phone back. "Marvel-Anne definitely had a unit just like that. It's not that weird that Kawamura has it. One of us might have left it in his vehicle. That happens sometimes."

"What is it worth?"

"Maybe a grand to replace it. Used, I wouldn't pay more than half that."

"So he's not financing his Venice high life by selling your gear."

"If it's ours, I'm sure he'll bring it on the next field trip."

Their food arrived, and Slater dug into it before he spoke again.

"Does Marvel-Anne have any connection to the arms trade?"

Ryan shook his head, setting down his burger. "Kawamura had the gun, not us."

"Is there any reason she'd have assault rifles?"

"Like military stuff? No way. Where is this coming from?"

"Something Frick and Frack said."

Ryan waved a hand. "Who?"

"The pair of Neanderthals at McInnes Shale Oil." Slater told him what had happened there, and how he'd got the black eye, and about the perfume bomb.

Ryan laughed. "I can't believe they thought you were walking around with a bottle of volatile high explosives."

"I can't believe that stuff is still in use. It seems like an old-timey kind of tool."

"That doesn't make it any less lethal."

After they'd eaten, Ryan looked tired. "I should return the Polara. If I'm not going back to La Mirada, I can take ride-shares."

"I'll tell Duarte. Where's the car?"

"It's parked on Sixth. A block or so that way." He waved toward the street. "At Broadway."

Slater pulled out his phone and thumb-typed a text to Duarte. While he had it in hand, he opened his email and deleted the dead-man message he'd composed to Max. A moment later Duarte's reply popped onto the screen.

"Duarte says he'll meet us at the Polara," he said, and tucked the phone away.

After Ryan had paid, they walked out to the street. The rain had stopped, but the asphalt glistened, and the air smelled clean. At the Polara, Ryan opened the trunk and pulled out his day pack.

As they waited on the sidewalk, Slater realized he was going to have to tell Duarte to pull the vehicle tracker. He wouldn't care that Slater had put it there, but if he found it himself, he'd want to know what it was. Those things weren't cheap—Slater wanted it back.

The familiar blue Impala pulled into the driveway in front of the Polara, and Duarte climbed out, wearing cargo shorts and a tan bowling shirt.

"Gentlemen," he called to them. "So how was it?"

Ryan handed him the keys. "It drives like a dream. I felt like a badass."

A smile spread across Duarte's face. "I'm glad."

"How much do I owe you?"

"Let's say two hundred. Unless you scratched it."

"I did not," Ryan said carefully, and slid the C-notes from his wallet.

As Duarte pocketed the cash, he said to Slater, "Thanks for the referral."

Slater shrugged. "I wasn't going to let him drive around in a Prius."

Duarte laughed at that, and climbed into the Polara. Slater walked with Ryan back to the Thunderbird, and they rode in silence together toward his apartment. He was tired, he realized. It had been a long day.

"The sex with you is getting better," Ryan said, interrupting his thoughts.

"Is that why you got wood outside the bar? It made me think you weren't taking me seriously."

"It's not that at all. It's just—you're hot."

"You're not being completely honest, though. You have to tell me what you want."

Ryan eyed him. "What do you mean?"

"Everybody has a sex thing. A turn-on. I think we're getting closer to yours."

He didn't respond to that, instead looking out at the dark wet city.

When they got upstairs, it took Slater a moment to find his front-door key. "I'm wiped out," he mumbled, by way of explanation.

"Do you just want to go to sleep?" Ryan said, as they stepped inside. He set his day pack on the carpet at the end of the sofa.

"I'll fuck you, Ryan, but we need to get at it."

He nodded. "I thought about what you said. About expressing what I want. I think maybe I'd like a nurturing type situation."

Slater put his hands on his hips. "You want Daddy to fuck you?"

Ryan winced. "That makes it sound so perverted. Isn't it kind of out of character for you?"

"With sex, there's no accounting." Slater watched him for a moment. "Come here."

When he stepped closer, Slater squeezed his biceps, then caressed his shoulders, and cradled his neck in his hands, and spoke softly.

"I'm proud of you."

"So we're doing this?" Ryan said.

Slater pulled back. "What do you think?" he demanded.

"OK. I get it. chill."

Ryan leaned in and kissed him, and Slater took his time with it, exploring his mouth and his neck. Grabbing his belt, Ryan pulled him closer, grinding his burgeoning woody into him.

Finally Slater pulled away. "Go get undressed, and get into bed."

Ryan took a deep breath and stepped toward the bedroom. As he went, Slater swatted him on the butt. A minute later he followed, and sat on the edge of the futon to untie his boots, then slid off his jeans. Ryan was naked, waiting for him, head propped on one arm.

Slater climbed beside him and ran a hand through his hair, then grabbed his cock, eliciting a gasp. Rolling away to grab the lube, he returned and held Ryan's gaze.

"My golden boy," Slater said, and slid his hand between his legs, and worked his way inside him. Mouthing his neck, eventually Slater reached for a condom. Pushing Ryan's knees up, he penetrated him as he stroked his cock. After a few minutes, Ryan cried out as he came, and that brought Slater to it at almost the same time. That didn't happen very often.

Not waiting even to catch his breath, Slater got up to guzzle his ration of bourbon, then went back to bed. With the warm golden glow in his belly, he was asleep before Ryan got back from the bathroom.

SIXTEEN

R YAN WAS GONE WHEN he woke in the morning. Scrabbling for his phone, he pulled up the tracking app and saw that he wasn't far away, at a coffee place on Vermont. It was nice to have the place to himself. He stretched out and dozed for a while longer.

The buzz of a text pulled him from his slumber. He grabbed his phone and saw that it was from Andy:

I have some results. You owe me $500.

How could a few minutes of typing on a computer be worth that much? He wrote back:

Ouch. I'll stop by soon.

Thinking about it, he sent a second text:

Chiseler.

Once he was dressed, he checked the wad of cash in the pocket of his jeans to make sure he had enough to pay Andy, and riffled five C-notes out of it. Downstairs in his garage, the Thunderbird had the space to itself again, and it looked comfortable, with plenty of air on both sides.

Slater backed into the alley and drove downtown, to a coffee place on Broadway near Andy's, and parked out front, pausing to feed the meter. Andy loved his java, and he ordered a Greek coffee for him and a soy latte for himself. Carrying both, he walked up the block to Andy's building.

When Andy pulled open the door, he beamed at the sight of the joe.

"You know what I like," he said, and took the smaller cup.

Slater followed him into the loft and dropped the stack of C-notes on the table.

"Your five dollars," he said. "I wouldn't mind getting the friends-and-family discount once in a while."

"I'm not a chiseler," Andy said, sitting at his desk and turning to face him. "My skills are … worth it."

Slater couldn't say anything to that, and watched as he slurped at the thick black coffee.

"The sweet taste of the old country," Andy said.

"You're not Greek."

"Not genetically. But in terms … of the java, I am."

"How did you get into Greek coffee? It's kind of hard to find."

"A Slovenian guy I knew used to … make it. He said you can draw a line on the map … of Europe, and on one side the coffee is Italian style, like it is here, and on the other … it's Greek. Apparently it's almost the same line where the … Byzantine Empire split. Anyway, I got addicted."

"You're the only person I know who could trace their coffee preferences to the Byzantine Empire," Slater said. "So what did you find out for my platinum-level fee?"

Andy took a slurp from the paper cup and then turned to his computer.

"Kawamura has a firearms license," he said. "Not just to carry, but to deal in them. Like a wholesaler, and … gun shows, stuff like that."

"Good to know," Slater said absently, and then met his gaze. "That's actually useful."

"Then there's this." Andy beckoned him over, and Slater stooped behind his shoulder to examine the screen. It showed several lines of text, like arcane database entries.

"What am I looking at?"

"A reservation for train tickets." Andy pointed a wavering finger at the screen. "Los Angeles

Union Station to Santa Fe, two tickets, tomorrow night. This one is your guy, Kawamura, and on the same reservation, sharing a double sleeping compartment, is Neva Dare, female." He turned to look at Slater. "Do you know her?"

"Neva Dare," Slater said, reading the name on the screen and then straightening up. "It's not *nee-vah*. It's *neh-vah*. 'Never there.' It's a pseudonym."

"Interesting that you can still … do that on the train. It's not like flying, where you need to have … an ID."

"You're a genius," Slater said.

"That's what I get paid for."

"Paid handsomely. But maybe you are worth it."

Swiveling around in his chair, Andy grabbed his belt buckle and tugged on it. "You should let me fuck you. I'll make you scream. It's been a while."

"We could do that." Slater took his hand, and interlaced their fingers. "I hope you're not going to phone it in, if you're all spent from riding sweaty Kyle."

"Ditch the jeans, punk. I'll show you … my A game."

Slater had to grin as he unbuttoned his shirt, and then slid off his jeans. Despite the big talk, he did most of the work when it came to sex with

Andy, as he lacked fine motor coordination. But Slater knew by now what to do, when to respond to his rhythmic random movements, when to present some resistance.

Andy wasn't wearing much, and in a second he was naked, and already hard. Slater let him push him backward onto the bed, and then Andy climbed on top of him, straddling his pelvis and grinding his woody into him.

Steadying him with one hand on his waist, Slater stroked him with the other. It didn't take him long. Andy craned upward and came with a yelp, a spasm shuddering through his body. Slater pulled him down and locked their mouths together as he stroked himself. Andy slid off and reached between his legs, probing him with his imprecise aim, his irregular pressure. It was a turn-on, and it sped things up. With his nose in Andy's hair, smelling the scent of his sweat, Slater climaxed.

After lying there for a minute, he got up and grabbed a towel, then handed it to Andy. Once they'd cleaned up, Slater stretched out behind him, and notched his knees behind Andy's, and wrapped an arm around his belly. This moment, the connection and the warmth and the feeling of satiety, was as good as it got.

Andy's breathing became rhythmic as he dozed off. Slater rolled to the other side and grabbed his phone, then propped himself up with the pillows. The tracking software showed that dick-smack Conrad was downtown today. As he zoomed in, he saw that the dot was inside one of the county courthouses. The idiot was probably giving evidence in a court case. Part of his job. But not even the thought of that moron could darken his mood today—Andy had just given him some information that might resolve Ryan's quest.

Checking on Ryan's location, he was at the Natural History Museum, and not just parked there—his phone was inside the building. What was he doing at that place for the third day in a row? No way was he secretly really into fossils.

Slater pulled up a map of the building. There were galleries on the first two levels, and administrative offices higher up. From the tracker, he could see what part of the structure the dot representing Ryan's phone was in, but it was impossible to tell what floor he was on.

As he got up to pull on his clothes, Andy woke. Slater buttoned his shirt and watched as he stretched, then cracked a smile as he met Slater's eye. Such a beautiful man.

Slater leaned in to kiss him. "Later, beautiful."

Out on Broadway, as he walked up on the Thunderbird, he saw a red-bordered slip of paper tucked under the wiper—a parking ticket. It was a stupid mistake—he should have moved the vehicle into a lot after he bought the coffee, but he'd forgotten.

"Fucking royal fuck," he muttered, stepping up and pulling it off the windshield.

"I can't take it back," a woman's voice said. "It's already in the system."

Slater turned to look toward the sidewalk. It was a parking enforcement officer, in her tan uniform, standing on the curb, her ticket machine in hand.

"Did I ask you to take it back?" he demanded.

She frowned. "Everyone always gets angry with me. I'm just doing my job."

"I'm not angry with you, toots. You got me dead to rights. I'm angry with myself—I know better than to let the meter run out."

Not waiting for a response, he climbed behind the wheel and tossed the citation on the passenger seat, eyeing the woman to make sure she wasn't going to ding him again if he lingered. But she was moving up the block, so he pulled out his phone and texted Max:

Can I use the Courier for a few hours?

His response came a moment later, before Slater pulled into the street:

It's all yours.

Slater drove to his own apartment and pulled

the Thunderbird into the garage, not bothering to roll the door down. He stayed just long enough to grab his bulky aluminum case and a pair of coveralls and load them into the trunk. The case was slender, like a briefcase, but it looked industrial, with exposed rivets and reinforced corners. He used it to transport sensitive stuff because it had a good solid lock, but hopefully it looked like the kind of box that might contain technical equipment.

From there he drove to Bunker Hill and Max's apartment. In the underground garage he opened his trunk and pulled on the coveralls and his blue ball cap, then drove the peppy little Courier out onto the street. He loved the tinny whine of the engine, the lightweight gearbox, and how responsive it was. Since Slater had introduced Max to Duarte, the vehicle was always in prime condition.

A few minutes later he pulled into the public lot at the Natural History Museum, and paid for parking, then cruised around to the side of the building where the map had shown the service entrance was. Slater grabbed his aluminum case and strode up to the guard, a chubby dark-haired guy in a security company uniform, seated behind a low desk.

Eyes glazed with boredom, the guard looked up and greeted him in Spanish.

"They called me about a LAN problem on the third floor," Slater said, resting the case on the edge of his desk.

"Is that for Monica?"

"I don't know who called, *vato*. I just go where I'm told."

He sat back in his chair. "I should call Monica."

"I don't know her, but I already know where the junction boxes are." He waved impatiently. "The museum is open, right? Maybe it would be faster if I just walked around to the public entrance."

The guy gave him the once-over, and for a moment Slater thought he was going to challenge him, but instead he gestured down the hall.

"The freight elevator is on the left."

Slater walked inside, suppressing a smile. Coveralls weren't really something that IT people wore, but they conveyed the message *I'm here to work,* and that was enough to grease the wheels.

The huge freight elevator was empty when the doors rumbled open for him. Slater punched the button for 3 and waited while the behemoth lumbered upward. When he stepped off into the hallway, he checked his phone. From here, the dot for Ryan's location was on the right. He walked in that direction and soon found himself in a vast dimly lit public gallery.

There were people here, couples and school-kids and their parents. Lining the walls were dioramas of desert and mountain and forest scenes, each with preserved animals posed as if they were alive. Slater had been here as a kid, but it felt different now—all the taxidermy made it like a morgue.

Obviously Ryan wasn't here. Slater had been aiming for the offices upstairs, but he'd under-shot by a floor or so. Walking back to where the freight elevator was, he found the stairwell and hustled up. In the hallway at the top was a set of double doors marked STAFF ONLY. When he pushed on one, it wasn't locked, and there was no one around to challenge him.

Checking his phone again, Ryan's position was ahead and on the left. In this hallway there was only one possibility on that side: a set of dou-ble doors with a sign above that read CONFER-ENCE ROOM B.

Briefly eyeing his phone again, Ryan was just a few yards ahead, likely inside this room. Slater hesitated. The guy was going to be pissed, and he'd have to explain how he found him, but he needed to know what he was up to. He took a deep breath and pulled open the door.

This was just an anteroom, a few feet deep, with another set of double doors at the end. With no locks or latches, they weren't for security, and had a narrow gap between them. Stepping close, he pulled off his ball cap and put it on backward, with the bill at the back of his neck, and leaned in to peer inside. At first all he could see was darkness.

Shifting position, he saw a trio of candle flames. It had to be a big room, because they were small, which meant they were some distance away. There were faces too, he realized, dimly illuminated by the flames, several of them in a circle. People sitting at a candlelit table. He could hear a woman's voice, but from here it was too muffled to make out the words. What the hell was going on?

Turning away to glance around the anteroom, Slater saw there was a lone light switch on the wall. He set down his aluminum case and flicked it off, plunging the space into darkness. When he pulled gently on one of the inner doors, it opened noiselessly, and he stepped into the room. No one seemed to notice—it was dark, and he wasn't anywhere near their table, and any inadvertent noise he might make was muted by the distant rattle of an air-conditioning vent with a loose vane.

As his eyes adjusted to the low light, he saw that there were seven people sitting around the table. In the dark it was impossible to tell how big the room was, but they were at least twenty feet from him. Scanning the dimly lit faces, he recognized a familiar profile—Ryan was among them.

"I need him to know that my anger is just one part of what we had," one of the women was saying. "There was also love. I'd appreciate it if he could just acknowledge that."

The group was silent for a moment, and then another woman spoke, her voice deeper, older.

"I'm not getting an explicit answer. I'm not actually certain that Teodoro is with us right now." She paused, and no one else said anything. The only sound came from the ventilation system. Finally she spoke again. "I am sensing a dark presence, however. Lurking nearby … It feels male in nature, and stealthy. Possibly malevolent. Observing us, and curious about us."

Slater felt a prickle at the back of his neck. It was a dead-on description of him—had she seen him come in?

The woman spoke again. "Perhaps Teodoro will communicate with us later. Moving on, Ryan—you had a question?"

The narrator's familiar voice spoke. "I was wondering about an incident that happened up the Washougal River not long ago. What were you trying to tell me? I saw the branches, and the weave, the intricacy of the patterns. It was beautiful. But I still don't understand."

He was talking to bigfoot, Slater realized. They were having a séance, and he was trying to get psychic vibes for his goddamn podcast. There was no need for Slater to listen to any more. He turned and pushed his way silently into the anteroom, and grabbed his case, then stepped out into the hall and headed for the freight elevator.

Riding downward, alone in the big car, he had to scoff. No surprise that Ryan was keeping that kind of research to himself. If he'd been up-front about it, though, Slater wouldn't have had to bluster his way in here. What a freaking waste of time.

On his way out, he nodded to the guard.

"Did you get it all straightened out?" the guy said.

"Good as new," Slater called back to him, not breaking his stride.

Once he was behind the wheel of the Courier, he saw that Conrad had texted.

Lunch? I'm downtown in court all day.

Slater thumb-typed a response:

Are you trying to lure me to the Civic Center to arrest me?

Conrad's reply came soon after:

No. Meet me at that pizza place.

Slater wrote back with his estimated arrival time, then started the high-revving little engine and drove to Max's apartment, nosing the pickup into the underground garage. Pulling off the coveralls, he rolled them up and ditched them in the trunk of the Thunderbird, along with the ball cap and the aluminum case, but then hesitated before he got behind the wheel. The Civic Center was right down the hill—he could walk there just as fast as driving, and there'd be no risk of getting another fat parking ticket.

No way would the bougie concierge on the front desk of Max's building let him inside again, so he took the garage door opener with him, and soon was out in the clean air, scrubbed fresh by last night's rain, and headed down the hill.

In his pants his phone rang, with the most annoying ring-tone of them all: *"No wire hangers! What's wire hangers doing in this closet when I told you no wire hangers—ever?"*

Slater picked up and demanded, "What do you need, woman?"

"I wanted to know what time you were going to stop by," Doris said.

He'd completely forgotten—probably because he didn't really want to deal with it.

"I'll need a couple hours," Slater said. "I couldn't find the right *Plumeria*. I'm going to stop at another nursery on the way over."

As he ended the call, he was walking up on the pizza place. Conrad wasn't here yet, he saw, stepping inside. Slater went to the counter to order, then found a table.

When Conrad strolled in, he was wearing civvies—black dress pants and a royal-blue shirt with a necktie. He waved when he spotted him, and flashed that easy smile. The guy was so even-tempered. Why was that so instantly irksome? Slater held up his little paper receipt, and Conrad nodded and went to order for himself. Such a great body. Even dressed like a bank teller, the way he filled out his clothes made Slater's stomach ache.

That smile, he wondered idly. Did that mean good news, or just that he was indifferent to Slater's legal troubles?

As Conrad sat down across from him, he pointed at Slater's eye. "It's a little darker today. At least it's not swollen."

"Are you down here giving evidence?"

"Eventually, I hope. There's no predicting when it'll happen. I might even have to come back Monday."

Slater waved impatiently. "Is the hippie dead?"

"Why do you say he's a hippie? I thought you didn't know him."

"He had a lot of hair. Lying on the carpet, he looked like a black-velvet painting of Jesus."

"Lucky for you, he's going to survive," Conrad said. "His name is Lance something-or-other. A small-time drug dealer."

"So nobody's looking for me." Slater took a deep breath.

"It doesn't mean you're not involved, though. Currently you're listed in the case file as witness Juan Doe number one."

"Because I phoned from there?" Slater said. "Why Juan?"

"You look more like a Juan than a John. They've got you on video. I was able to watch it. It's pretty low resolution, so they can't really see your face."

"I didn't see a camera in there."

"It was hidden in a banker's box behind the desk. He's a drug dealer, right? No surprise he had surveillance."

"Fuck me," Slater muttered.

The waiter stepped up with their pizzas and set them down. Conrad tucked in before he spoke, munching with gusto.

"It's obvious in the video what you did. You checked on him and then called it in—nothing illegal about that. Although wiping your prints off the horn was a little suspicious. In any case, nobody wants to track you down."

"That means they know who flattened him?"

"Lance is still too messed up to make a statement, and he probably won't rat on them anyway. But it's on the video—a man and a woman. The name you had was extremely useful."

"It was Norma López?"

"And her boyfriend, apparently. The boyfriend did the beat-down, and a few minutes later you show up. They probably thought they'd iced him, but Lance got lucky."

"It wasn't just a conflict that escalated," Slater said, and threw down a chunk of crust. "They left a message earlier in the day—it was something they'd planned ahead."

"Based on the video, the prosecutor is going with that. Premeditated attempted murder."

Slater scoffed. "Norma wanted me to take the fall."

"You or your client," Conrad said, waving a half-eaten slice. "Whoever that is."

"That's confidential."

"Anyway, you can wash your hands of it. Forgive and forget. We got both of them. Norma's in jail right now eating baloney sandwiches."

"I'll find forgiveness when they pull her cold lifeless body out of the gas chamber."

Conrad frowned. "It won't be a death-penalty case. And no one's been executed in California in decades."

"You know what I mean." Folding his arms, Slater sat back. "I wish I could express my gratitude, or whatever it is that normies are supposed to do. I'm not very good at that stuff."

"It balances out," Conrad said. "I kept you out

of it, and you gave us the perp's name. That saved a detective a lot of legwork."

"Still." He gestured helplessly.

"You don't have to say anything. Maybe just help me out sometime. My palm tree needs some work."

"The one in your backyard? What's wrong with it?"

"It's got all those dead fronds hanging down."

"You freaking moron," Slater snapped. "That's a fire hazard. What is wrong with you?"

"There's the Slater I know," Conrad said, and threw up his hands.

"Did you just forget, or are you willfully trying to harm that tree?"

"When you get some time, come out and have a look." Conrad checked his watch. "I have to get back to sitting on a hard bench outside a courtroom." He rose and met his eye. "Take care of yourself."

Slater scoffed. "I always do."

After he'd wiped his hands, he followed him out to the street, and walked back up Bunker Hill. He felt lighter knowing that he wasn't going to have to deal with anything concerning the hippie. It was actually to his advantage that the guy had surveillance—it exonerated him, and put Norma López and her enforcer in the can. She'd only met Ryan once, and must have figured he was suitably innocent, not connected to her business, not even a local guy. She'd used him as the patsy. A convenient civilian to frame up.

The whole thing reinforced exactly why Slater worked alone. If he'd gone to interview Norma himself, she wouldn't have dared to attempt a setup like that. Letting Ryan deal with these people was a mistake. The guy wasn't stupid, but he was cerebral, and outdoorsy, and a little clueless, not equipped for the depths of the cesspool.

Walking into Max's garage, he climbed in the Thunderbird and headed to Mount Washington. The nursery that was on the way was in Cypress Park, under the big electric transmission lines. Driving toward it, he passed the end of Roseview Walk. It felt odd to be here again—like he was doing something wrong, or tempting fate.

At the nursery he walked around and found some *Plumeria* saplings in black plastic pots. He inspected the leaves and picked one that looked healthy, then paid for it and set it on the floor of the passenger side of his car.

In Doris's driveway, as he walked around to unload it, she came out to greet him, grasping his forearms and leaning in to kiss his cheek. As she pulled back, she frowned, and kept hold of his arms.

"What happened to your eye?"

"I fell on the stairs."

Doris put her hands on her hips. "Try again."

Slater sighed. "I was interviewing an oilman, and he didn't like my questions. It was a simple scuffle." He pulled the *Plumeria* sapling out of the car, but she ignored it.

"Why didn't you tell me you were on *Ooh, No She Didn't*?"

"That was on already?" Slater set the pot down and straightened up. "Why are you watching that low-brow garbage?"

"I don't watch it. One of my girlfriends does, and she recognized you. I found it archived online."

"This case with Ryan has been kind of nuts. I took the job as security to get close to the producer, so I could interview her. She thought I looked the part."

"You looked good, in the few moments you were on the screen." Her brow furrowed. "But all the fighting. I didn't raise you to be a pugilist."

"Well, that's what you got."

Doris eyed the *Plumeria*. "Can I pay you for the bush?"

"It's a tree. You don't have to pay for it, but you could do me a favor." He counted out three twenties from his wad of cash and then grabbed the parking ticket from the passenger seat. "Can you pay that? It's sixty-three. I owe you three bucks, plus a stamp."

"What, you don't have your own checks?" Doris said.

"I could probably get them. I mostly work in cash."

"I'll take care of it," she said, and tucked it into her hip pocket.

Slater picked up the *Plumeria* and carried it into the backyard.

"We'll plant it on higher ground, like you said. You pick the spot."

Setting the pot down, he went to the shed to get a spade and a trowel, and pulled on a pair of gardening gloves. When he got back, Doris had carried the pot to a spot at the side of the yard.

"How about here?" she said, pointing to the ground next to her. "Is it too sunny?"

"It'll need lots of sun," he said, and drove the spade into the earth with his boot, lifting out the soil.

Doris stood back. "It looks rocky."

"That's what we want. It needs good drainage."

She watched him, arms folded. "Your father would have loved this yard. He would have loved what you've done with it."

"Did he have a green thumb?"

"Not really. But he would have loved the idea that you do."

Once the hole was deep enough, Slater threw in a handful of fertilizer and churned it into the soil with the tip of the spade. Next he ran the hose into it for a while, then lifted the sapling from its black plastic pot, glad to see that the roots weren't too dense. He spent a minute massaging the packed earth around the roots to loosen it, then set the plant in the hole he'd dug.

"We never talk about him," he said, avoiding Doris's gaze.

"You know he loved you."

"I hardly remember." With the trowel, he shoveled dirt from the pile into the space around the root ball.

"I want you to remember," she said.

Part of him did, he knew, in his irrational reaction, the lump that had formed in his throat. Slater got to his feet.

"If we're planting this together, you need to move some dirt."

Doris knelt and grabbed the trowel, scooping earth around the sapling and tamping it down.

"In memory of your father," she said.

After the soil was in place, Slater picked up the hose and gave it a good soaking.

"Does it need that much water?" Doris said, watching him work.

"Just the first day. To get it established. After that, it's pretty drought-tolerant. It won't need to be flooded again."

After he put the tools away, Doris put an arm

around his waist, and they walked toward the house.

"Stay for dinner?" she said. "Albert might be back."

"I have to work."

"Well, this is a lovely memorial."

"It should thrive there," Slater said, and leaned down to kiss her. "Love you."

Once he was in his car, he checked the location tracker on Ryan's phone. He was downtown, in the central library. Slater sent him a text:

Where are you?

His reply came a moment later:

Downtown. Want to eat?

Slater texted him the name of a bar that had Mexican food. It was just a few blocks from the library.

SEVENTEEN

S LATER PARKED ON SEVENTH and made sure he fed the meter enough that it wouldn't expire. There was no sign of Ryan outside the bar. Walking in, the place was crowded and noisy, the booze-fueled conversations of the diners echoing off the ancient tin ceiling. Ryan was at a table by the wall, reading a menu. He walked over and pulled out the opposite chair.

"Last time you waited outside," Slater said as he sat down.

"I thought if I came in, there'd be less chance that you'd slap me."

"Technically, that was a kovac. I thought you'd set me up. You needed a kovac."

"I didn't set you up. You know that," he said,

then sat back, and sighed. "So how is a kovac different from a slap?"

"It's about the double action," Slater said. "In Japan it's called *oufuku binta*, a round-trip slap. Some lowlifes call it the paintbrush, and a cop I know called it the Joan Crawford. She used to do that in her movies."

Ryan chuckled. "You have a unique area of expertise. So what's good here?"

"Burritos, or any of the plates."

A waiter in a black shirt came over and took their order.

"Bring us a couple margarita rocks too," Slater told him.

"Does that fit with your booze rules?" Ryan said, once the waiter was gone.

"Sure it does—I'm still working, but it's only one, and I'm with someone."

"It sounds complicated."

"So can you find out where Kawamura is without making him suspicious?" Slater said.

"Why?"

"I want to get into his rental when he's not around."

"Why would you do that?"

"I think Kawamura knows more than he told me. I found out that he's the armaments guy, not Marvel-Anne. But Marvel-Anne is the one who sold the assault rifles to that oil company."

Ryan frowned. "Do you think they're collaborating?"

"It's a possibility."

"She wouldn't do that to me," he said intently.

Slater paused as the waiter set down their drinks, then clinked his glass against Ryan's.

"So let's get more information," Slater said.

Concern furrowing his brow, Ryan slurped at his margarita before he spoke. "I do owe him money. It's an easy excuse to get him to meet me, and have a beer. He's a craft-brew connoisseur."

"Great. There's a brewpub near here on Broadway. That would get him away from Venice. It has to be tonight or early tomorrow."

"What's the name of the place? I'll call him now." Ryan dug in his pants pocket.

Slater pulled up the listing for the brewpub on his phone, and set it on the table facing him.

"Hey, bud," Ryan said, holding his own phone to his ear. "It wasn't about insurance. He works in insurance, but I hired him to help me find Marvel-Anne. ... How can you blame me for that? Did he punch you or something?" He eyed Slater. "He hasn't really turned up anything yet. ... Listen, I owe you some money. Do you have time to get a drink tonight? I can pay you. ... I'm taking a break from that right now. I don't really know anyone in this burg. ... There's actually a fun brewpub in downtown LA. It's on Broadway." He looked at Slater's phone and recited the address. "See you then."

The waiter arrived with their food, and Slater picked up his margarita and slammed the rest of it.

"I'm meeting him in an hour," Ryan said.

"Excellent." Slater eyed him over the plates. "Do not tell him what we know. About the weapons or the oil company."

"Of course not."

"And don't drink too much. Otherwise you might let slip about Norma López or Im Hae. Kawamura doesn't need to know about any of that."

Ryan frowned. "Sure thing, Dad."

"That's not what you said last night."

He chuckled, and then blushed, and focused on his enchiladas. When they were done eating, Slater rose.

"I need to get moving," he said, and dug his cash out of his pocket.

"Put your money away," Ryan said. "I'll buy you dinner."

"Text me when Kawamura gets there."

<hr>

SLATER DROVE TO HIS apartment, and parked in his garage, and waited for the door to roll down. Unlocking his armored cabinet, he grabbed the lock reader and the binder of keys. The gear went in the trunk, and then he hit the button to roll up his garage door, and started the Thunderbird.

Aiming for the freeway, he drove west, toward the beach. The last rays of the setting sun glared from the horizon, and he pulled down the visor as he navigated the sluggish traffic.

Ryan's text came as he was trolling for parking near Kawamura's rental:

He's here.

Finally finding an open space on a side street, he pulled in, then grabbed a pair of black latex gloves from the box in the backseat and wriggled into them. He stuffed the lock probe in his hip pocket, and set off toward Kawamura's rental.

Twilight was fading as he walked up on the big glassy house. The garage door was completely closed now. He knew Kawamura would take the Mercedes downtown. There were no lights on, he saw, gazing upward. The place was likely empty— it would be hard to lay low with all that glass.

At the gate into the tiny yard, Slater reached over and found the chain to unlatch the door, then went in and closed it gently behind him. A quick look around for cameras revealed none.

Pulling the lock reader from his pocket, he connected it to his phone. The screen went black and said "готов." As he slid the slender probe into the lock on the front door, the phone went red and flashed "ошибка." Slater didn't know that word, but he knew the red screen meant it wasn't working.

Do not fail on me now. He adjusted the probe, twisting it slightly and then sliding it out a little, and then it worked—the screen went green and displayed 334.

Exiting the yard, Slater strode back to his car and opened the trunk. He glanced over his shoulder to make sure he wasn't being observed, then flipped open the binder, turning the heavy pages, and slid the key out of the pouch labeled 334. Digging in a small duffel bag of tools he kept next to the spare tire, he found a mini flashlight. There was so much glass in that place, he didn't want to risk turning on the room lights.

Back at Kawamura's rental, he let himself through the gate and then tried the key in the front door. It twisted freely, retracting the deadbolt, and he stepped inside. The alarm panel was lit up and said FRONT DOOR OPEN, but it wasn't reporting that to anyone—when he closed the door, it said DISABLED, as it had yesterday. There was no danger from a disconnected alarm, no matter what it knew about the doors.

Gazing up the stairs into the darkness, he called out, "Maintenance," and listened for a moment. "Hello," he called, louder this time. There was no response, no sound—no one was here.

Once he'd climbed the stairs, he found he was in a big open room, with glass on three sides. At one end was a modern kitchen, and at the other a living room. More than enough ambient light came in through the windows for him to see the layout. Four white stools lined the marble-topped kitchen island. The lounge furniture was white too, and the walls were all paneled in wood. It felt stark, but this must be the current trend in pretentious housing.

Clicking on his flashlight, he checked in the kitchen alcove, and then the little bathroom near the top of the stairs. There was no personal stuff, just the generic art and towels and accoutrements that came with the rental.

Behind the fireplace another staircase led upward, and when he climbed it, he found a couple of bedrooms. One of them was untouched, the bed still made, but the other looked lived in, with clothes strewn on the floor, the sheets rumpled and askew. The closet door was ajar, and the beam of his flashlight revealed two suitcases inside, both standing upright. He lifted each of them. Both were empty, and one had a paper label looped through the handle that read SEA and LAX along with a flight number, but neither one had ID tags.

On the floor next to them was a smaller case,

made of hard black plastic. It had a combination lock on it, but when he picked it up, it was open. On the inside, the molded plastic bore the vague outline of a handgun. This was Kawamura's gun safe. He'd need this for flying with his weapon.

Next to the closet was a dresser, and he rolled open the top drawer. Kawamura had unpacked—it contained T-shirts and stretchy men's underpants. Judging by the size, they were definitely his.

When he opened the next drawer and pulled out a pair of jeans, unfolding them to look them over, a smile slowly spread across his face. These didn't belong to that guy. They were cut to fit a curvy woman. Slater knew who it was—Neva Dare, Kawamura's bunkmate for tomorrow night's train trip. More widely known as Marvel-Anne. Based on the photo of her that Ryan had shown him, these clothes were right. It had to be her.

In the drawer next to the jeans were some girly button-up blouses and rolled-up T-shirts. That had come up in the podcast, he remembered—when they were packing their backpacks to head into the forest, Ryan and Marvel-Anne talked about the utility of rolling their shirts rather than folding them.

Flapping open one of the T-shirts to get a look at it, he saw that it was also cut for a buxom woman. The front was silk-screened with the silhouette of a loping bigfoot along with two

Chinese characters: 成功. Slater spread the shirt out on the end of the bed, then photographed it with his phone. Zooming in on the Chinese characters, he photographed them up close, then copied the image to a translation app. In a moment it told him what the characters meant: "success."

He rerolled the shirt into a tight tube and tucked it into the back of his belt. Tangible evidence was much more powerful than any photo he could show Ryan. But Marvel-Anne might notice it was missing. Slater considered that for a moment. He'd have to stage a burglary.

Pulling her clothes out of the drawer by the handful, he dumped them on the floor, then did the same with Kawamura's shirts and shorts. In the next drawer he pulled out a pair of pants, then stopped when he saw what was beneath them—a blue velvet box. He popped it open. It was a case for jewelry. The stuff looked like it belonged to a woman. It also looked real—a double strand of pearls, some diamond earrings and bracelets, a showy heart-shaped pendant studded with blue and white gemstones.

"Damn it," he muttered. A real thief would take all this, but he couldn't. He closed the box and put it back where it had been, then folded the pants and put them on top, arranging them the way he'd found them. He rolled that drawer closed, but left the upper ones open. Hopefully

Marvel-Anne would assume the thief had stopped after rifling a couple of drawers, and had given up before finding the truly valuable stuff.

Next he pulled the sheets off the bed and tossed the pillows in a corner. In the attached bathroom, he opened the cabinet and found a shaving kit, and dumped it into the sink. Too bad there were no prescriptions—those were easy to carry, and junkies always stole the medications, no matter what they were.

As he stepped back into the bedroom, he heard a sound downstairs. He clicked off his flashlight and froze. A door closing. It was two flights down, but the sound was unmistakable. The front door.

Checking his phone, there was nothing from Ryan. It was way too soon for Kawamura to be back. That meant it was the owner of the girly clothes—Marvel-Anne.

Slater listened intently, not moving, and eyed the windows. Somewhere below he heard footsteps on the stairs, then the sound of the television. She was on the floor below, but she wasn't coming up here just yet.

Stepping over to the big window, he gingerly slid it open, then popped out the screen. It detached from the frame with a metallic *snap*. Slater paused to listen again, but with the TV on, she wouldn't have heard that. He tossed the screen on the bed. It was at least twenty feet down to the dark narrow space between the house and the high fence, he saw, leaning out, and there was nothing for him to jump on.

A narrow ledge, less than a foot wide, ran along the bottom of the window, and as he craned farther out, he saw that it ran the length of the structure, to the tiny yard near the front door, where a lone tree grew, some kind of *Ficus,* its branches stretching up beyond the eaves. The question now was whether the ledge was a decorative detail or a structural element that would bear his weight. There was only one way to find out.

Stepping out the window, he put his boot on the ledge and sat on the sill, gradually shifting his weight onto that foot. It felt solid. Swinging his other leg outside, he carefully stood erect, with his back to the open window. His heart was pounding, and he took a deep breath to calm himself. He could almost see the beach from here. Focused on his feet, he took a step sideways, his back to the wall now, and a few steps later he was brushing along a stretch of glass. Another sidestep, and another. Gradually he got to the end of the structure, managing to maintain his balance.

The *Ficus* was within reach now. It looked healthy. If he could propel himself into the middle of it, the branches should hold his weight. There wasn't enough room to crouch and increase his reach before he jumped, so Slater took a breath to steel himself, then let his body fall forward a little as he bent his knees, then pushed off and leaped into the heart of the tree, grabbing at the branches. He couldn't get a grip at first, but the foliage slowed him down, and he landed upright, astride a thick bough halfway to the ground. There was light inside the windows here at his new eye level, he saw, the living room or the kitchen, but the curtains were drawn.

He'd scraped his forearm, and one of his gloves was shredded, but his palms weren't cut up. Suddenly it felt like he'd been on the wrong end of a dick punch. He'd landed on his junk, he realized. He struggled with the pain, trying to breathe as he winced and doubled over.

Eventually he'd recovered enough to move. Pulling himself up, he swung his leg around the branch and sought a foothold farther down. It took a few minutes, but eventually he climbed far enough down to hop to the ground. His jeans were dirty now, and one shirtsleeve was ripped, but he was in one piece.

Letting himself out the gate, he closed it gently and scanned the street. No one was around to witness his grubby tattered state—they were all ensconced in their nouveau gilded-age fortresses, their inertia actively sterilizing the creative bohemian vibe that had attracted them here.

He swatted some dust off himself, and ran a hand through his hair, and took a deep breath as he walked toward the boulevard.

As SLATER CLIMBED INTO his car, he felt a lump in the back of his pants. Reaching around, he pulled out the T-shirt he'd taxed from the bedroom drawer. Good thing he hadn't dropped it in that tree. He sent Ryan a text:

I'm finished. You can cut Kawamura loose.

Traffic had lightened up by the time he got on the freeway, and it didn't take long to get back to Westlake. Once he was in his garage, he threw the pilfered T-shirt in the trunk of his car, then headed upstairs. There was no sign of Ryan, and he hadn't responded to his text.

Slater got undressed, ditching his jeans in the bottom of the closet and his torn shirt in the kitchen trash. He massaged his thigh where he'd slammed it—it felt like it was going to bruise, but at least the skin wasn't broken. He took a long shower and then stretched out in his recliner with his phone.

The tracker for Ryan showed that he had left the brewpub, but he hadn't gone far, just up the street. Zooming in on the map, Slater realized he knew the place—Ryan was at Agatha's Bells. It was a dance bar for energetic young guys. He'd definitely be popular there.

That seemed kind of selfish, going out dancing when Slater was literally busting his ass on this job. He had a lot to tell Ryan—he'd cracked the case, and had hard evidence now about where Marvel-Anne was and what she was doing. There should be some satisfaction in that, a sense of achievement, but staring at the dot on the map, all he felt was annoyed.

If Ryan was at that wild dance club, there was no telling when he'd be back. No way was Slater going to wait around for him. Pushing himself out of the recliner, he went to the kitchen and pulled out the fifth of bourbon. He slammed his ration, and then guzzled some extra from the bottle. He'd fallen through a damn *Ficus* tonight— he deserved a bonus. Once he'd killed the lights, he put on the radio, Friday-night house music, and settled into the recliner again.

Sometime later he woke to the sound of someone trying to get the front door open. Before he could move, it flew open, and the room lights came on. Wincing at the sudden brightness, Slater sat up.

As he stepped inside, Ryan slammed the door. "Hey, man. Why are you naked?"

Slater looked him over, his lip curling in disgust. "You're blotto."

"Just a little," he said, his voice loud, and held out an unsteady thumb and forefinger. "So what did you find at Kawamura's crib?"

"We'll talk about that tomorrow."

"Is it bedtime?" he said, his eyes narrowing.

"First, you need to drink some water. Two or three glasses. As much as you can keep down."

Ryan sighed and went to the kitchen sink. Slater got into bed, watching as Ryan came in and fumbled with his clothes, clumsily getting undressed.

"Did you get tanked with Kawamura?" Slater said.

"I started with Kawamura, and then it was all the boys in town." He made a sweeping gesture, tossing his shirt on the floor.

"You found Agatha's Bells."

Ryan frowned. "How did you know?"

"It's close to where you were headed."

Once Ryan was naked, he killed the light and climbed onto the futon with Slater, draping a hand across his belly. Slater shifted his arm under his neck. His skin was damp and hot, and he could smell the cloying sweet tang of the booze on him.

"I don't think it's going to work," Ryan said, making a slow circle with his palm.

"What's not going to work?"

"You and me. You're too urban, Slater."

"Is that a euphemism for dark-skinned?"

"It means you're part of this crazy city. I need to be out in the woods, you know?"

"Yeah. I know."

EIGHTEEN

Sunlight was streaming in the filmy bedroom window when Slater woke. Ryan had roused him, he realized, when he sat up in bed.

"How bad?" Slater said, resting his palm on his lower back.

"My head hurts."

"Is the room spinning?"

"No."

"Then it's not that bad."

Slater got up and went to the bathroom, and brought back a couple of ibuprofen tablets, and a glass of water from the kitchen. Ryan looked rough, sitting on the edge of the futon, hunched over, his face screwed up like he was nauseous. He took the tablets and popped them in his mouth, and slammed the water, then hiccupped.

"Get dressed," Slater said, watching him. "We're going for breakfast."

"I don't think I can face that right now."

"It's the best thing for a hangover."

He herded Ryan down to the garage, then drove to a diner on Vermont. On the way, Ryan slouched in the passenger seat, shielding his eyes from the daylight with his hand.

The restaurant was busy on Saturday morning, but they managed to get a table. Inside, Slater ordered a quesadilla for him, and oatmeal for himself, and coffee for them both. By the time he'd finished, Ryan was still eating, chewing slowly on the greasy tortilla.

"Let me get something from my car," Slater said, and got up.

When he came back, he handed over the Sasquatch T-shirt. Ryan set down his coffee cup and folded it open.

"Where did you get this?" he said.

"Is it hers?"

"You found her," he said intently. "Where is she?"

"That was in a drawer at Kawamura's rental."

Ryan stared at him. "Then he took it from her. Marvel-Anne must have left her laundry bag in his car. Or Kawamura went digging in her backpack." He scowled. "That pervert."

Slater shook his head. "There were other girl clothes, and jewelry. She's staying there. They're sharing a bedroom."

"Why?" he demanded. His face contorted. "What is she doing with him?"

"They're working together. Marvel-Anne sold some rifles to those oil industry lowlifes, probably because she knew people in the business. Kawamura has the armaments license to sell them."

"I saw him last night. He told me he hadn't talked to her since our last excursion. Up the Washougal River."

"He lied to you," Slater said. "My researcher found that they have train tickets booked for tonight. Two berths in a double compartment. They're going to New Mexico."

Ryan raised his voice. "Why?"

"I have no idea."

"I need to talk to her. I'm going over there."

"We'll go together."

"I can handle those two on my own," he said firmly, and pulled out his phone. "What's the address?"

"Things have changed," Slater said. "Think about it. This isn't a walk in the woods. The pair of them are selling assault rifles."

Ryan stared at him, doubt creeping into his eyes. There were dark shadows beneath his brow, and he looked pale and tired, still suffering from the hangover.

"This kind of stuff is my world, not yours," Slater said. "You hired me because I know how to navigate it. Let me do my job."

He sighed. "I guess maybe you should come."

"I should. And for your own safety, you have to do exactly what I say."

Ryan nodded absently and slumped back. Slater signaled the waiter for the check, and once he'd paid, led Ryan out to the parking lot.

"Do you have any more painkillers?" Ryan said, climbing in the passenger side.

"You've had enough. Take slow deep breaths. The food will make you feel better soon."

Slater got on the freeway and headed west, navigating the sluggish traffic toward Venice. Ryan sat with his arms folded, intermittently dozing and gazing out at the city, a sullen look on his face. Exiting onto surface streets, Slater drove into the neighborhood and found a place to park just a few houses up from Kawamura's rental. He killed the engine.

"That's the place," he said, pointing out the house to Ryan.

"That's where they're staying?" he demanded. "Is that a GLS in the garage? I don't pay them that well."

"They're arms dealers now, remember?" Slater

dug in the pocket of his jeans and found the key labeled 334. "This is the front door key. I'll text you in a few minutes, when I'm ready for you. Reach over the gate and pull the chain to open it. This will unlock the front door to the house. We'll be on the second floor."

"How do you have a key to this place?" Ryan demanded.

"Don't ask me that."

"Why wouldn't I just ring the bell? And how are you going to get in? Can't we go in together?"

"Just do what I say. Wait until I text."

The nose of the Mercedes was sticking out of the garage, and Slater climbed out of the Thunderbird and walked over, ducking under the half-open door. His assumption panned out—at the back, the door into the foyer was still unlocked. These two were so careless. Even though they'd been burgled last night, they were still leaving the place vulnerable.

"Hello," Slater called up the stairs. He heard movement, and not pausing, he hustled up, taking the steps two at a time.

Kawamura was at the top, sitting on one of the stools at the kitchen island, not wearing his suit jacket but with his harness on, his weapon visibly holstered under his arm. As Slater appeared, he slid off the stool and stepped toward him.

"What are you doing here?" Kawamura

frowned. "How did you get in?"

"Hey, big guy," Slater said, and flashed a smile. "The door was open. I called, but I guess you didn't hear me." Stepping up to him, he clapped Kawamura on the shoulder.

"It was open?" Kawamura said, his brow furrowing.

"How are you doing?" Slater said, and pulled him closer, almost into a chest-bump. At the same time, with his other hand, he reached for the sidearm, and yanked it out of its holster. Stepping back, he leveled the weapon at Kawamura's chest.

Startled at first, Kawamura's expression shifted when he realized what had just happened. He shot Slater a murderous glare.

"You freaking little weasel."

"Don't feel bad," Slater said. "Martial arts people never anticipate the bro-hug move. It's not part of your culture. If I'd pranced in here waving a sword around, I'm sure you would have had the upper hand." He waggled the weapon. "Have a seat."

Kawamura didn't budge. Slater could see the wheels turning, as he considered what Slater might do, and calculated how risky it was to rush him. Not taking his eyes off the guy, Slater pulled on the weapon's slider, audibly chambering a round.

"Don't make me ask again," he said intently, and raised his eyebrows.

Moving back to the kitchen island, Kawamura sat on one of the stools. Standing on the other side of the island, with the weapon still aimed at him, Slater called toward the fireplace, where the stairs led to the upper floor.

"Come on out, Marvel-Anne. We need to talk."

A moment later, she stepped out of the stairwell. Marvel-Anne was an imposing figure, he saw, tall as well as curvy. Today she was wearing jeans, and an airy black top, and her dark-rimmed glasses.

Marvel-Anne waved an arm. "Who the hell are you?"

"Ryan hired me to track you down," Slater said. "I've been talking to your friends and associates all week. You're a complicated woman." He waved the weapon. "Have a seat."

She walked over to the island and pulled out the stool beside Kawamura.

"The one at the end," Slater said.

She scowled and moved away from Kawamura, taking the seat farthest from him.

Kawamura folded his arms. "This is technically kidnapping, bro. You could go away for a long time."

"I'm not the one who brought the heater, Stretch," Slater said. He eyed Marvel-Anne. "So—all roads lead to Santa Fe."

"What are you talking about?"

"You know—the Santa Fe Trail, the road to California, the inland Camino Real from Mexico City. Santa Fe, the fabled crossroads of the Southwest. Everything converges on that little plaza. Including you two. You're headed there this evening." He frowned. "You know, I've never taken a train trip. It sounds relaxing."

"That has nothing to do with Ryan," she said flatly. "Do you know what at-will employment means? I can leave whenever I want. I'm not under contract, I'm not indentured, and I don't owe him anything. It's none of his business what I do."

Slater turned to Kawamura. "Are you involved with the assault rifles, or is that just her gig?"

"I don't know what you're talking about," he said.

"You're a good liar, I'll give you that. You had Ryan snowed. The thing I don't get is why the two of you are keeping silent with him. It has to be more than the conclusion of your at-will employment."

Frowning at him, Marvel-Anne folded her arms.

Slater waved the pistol. "I'm asking you a question. Sing, sister."

"Why are you working for Ryan?" she demanded.

"He's paying me."

"Why would we tell you anything?"

"Because I'm the one with the rod."

She scowled, and looked away.

"You know, you've already told me a lot," Slater said.

It was a manipulative thing to say, but it worked—Marvel-Anne couldn't contain her curiosity, and took the bait.

"Like what?"

"Well, you said 'we,' which means you two are together romantically, I'm thinking. Did Ryan know that?"

"You don't know what he's really like," Kawamura said.

"You said that before. Lay it out for me—what is he really like?"

"Controlling," Marvel-Anne said. "He's the boss of everything. Of both of us. We needed to escape his gravity."

"You seem like you can take care of yourself. I know you got through grad school, and you brokered that assault-rifle deal with the chumps at McInnes Shale Oil." Slater gestured to Kawamura. "And you're strutting around armed all the time. It's not easy to control the guy who's packing heat. How could Ryan be a threat to either of you?"

"It's emotional, not physical," she said. "Have

you spent any time with him? Ryan is so sensitive. It was easier for everyone just to make a clean break. I didn't want to hurt him."

"Why? Were you romantic partners?"

She frowned. "Hell, no. He's gay."

"Me neither," Kawamura said. "I don't do guys. It was a business relationship, but it was emotionally fraught. We were isolated together for long periods. Just the three of us, out in the forest, with no way to connect to the outside world. You can imagine how intense that could get."

"I'm getting a mixed message here," Slater said. "Ryan is controlling and you're afraid of him, or Ryan is sensitive and you're protecting him. Which is it?"

"Both," Marvel-Anne said. "The three of us are emotionally entangled in the work. Days turn into weeks. Weeks become months. The quest is endless."

"You don't think the Sasquatch is real?" Slater said.

Her eyes narrowed. "Of course it's real."

"We've all seen more than enough evidence," Kawamura said. "We've heard the creature. There's no doubt in my mind that it's out there."

"But you're giving up on the search."

Marvel-Anne gestured impatiently. "All the work we've done has led me to the conclusion that the nature of bigfoot transcends the boundary between the real world and the metaphysical. It inhabits that liminal space. I know now that we'll never get more than a blurry photo, a cry in the night, a tuft of hair—because that's what it wants."

"So you want to disentangle from Ryan, and from the quest," Slater said. "Why didn't you just tell him that?"

"You know," Kawamura said, "the most stable emotional structure is a tripod. It's so hard to pull out of it, because if you do, the other legs collapse."

"In this case, though, you're both pulling out. That leaves just the one leg." He sighed. "So what's with the assault rifles?"

"How do you know about that, anyway?" Marvel-Anne said.

"Just answer the damn question."

"That's mostly me," Kawamura said. "It's certainly none of your business, but it's not a secret either. I bought several of them at an auction. I have a license to do that. It's all legal."

"I don't care about what's legal," Slater said. "I'm not John Law. Why are you selling them here and not in Oregon?"

"This is where the market is." He gestured expansively. "I wanted to raise some cash for us to live on for a while. Marvel-Anne knew people who needed firepower."

"Buy them cheap, mark them up, sell them

on," Slater said. "Like cans of soup or T-shirts."

"My margin is a lot higher than the markup on soup."

Slater watched him for a moment. "I guess I buy that." He eyed Marvel-Anne. "Did you know that Norma López is a drug dealer?"

"I haven't heard that name in a while. Norma was a wild one—it doesn't surprise me. Where did you find her?"

"I never actually met the woman, but she tried to frame me for killing another drug dealer. It backfired—she's the one who wound up in the hoosegow." Slater waved the weapon. "Long story. So if you're not doing anything illegal, why did you use a fake name on the train ticket?"

"I didn't want Ryan to find me."

"Buying a train ticket in another city is pretty obscure. How could he have found you?"

"You managed to," she said sharply, "even with the alias."

"Listen," Kawamura said. "We're not doing anything wrong. We need to cut the cord from *Sasquatch Search* and make a fresh start. Ryan needs to reinvent himself too."

"Separately from us," Marvel-Anne added.

"That's easy for you," Slater said. "Not so much for him. You're acting like thieves in the night. He's completely clueless. Why didn't you just tell him what you were doing?"

"He'll be fine." Marvel-Anne scoffed. "Ryan is like a cork in water. No matter how much you push him down, he bounces right back up again."

"Still, there's nothing worse than not knowing. You have to tell him what's going on."

From downstairs came the sound of the front door opening, and then footsteps on the stairs. Kawamura eyed Slater and frowned.

"What the hell?" Marvel-Anne demanded. "Burglars, and this thug, and now someone else. Does the lock on that door not work?"

Ryan appeared at the top of the stairs, breathing hard. His eyes shone with rage.

"You were supposed to wait," Slater said.

Ryan ignored him, staring at Kawamura and Marvel-Anne. "So it's true." He stepped toward the island and raised his voice. "How could you do this to me?"

Both of them looked away—Marvel-Anne pressed her mouth into a hard line, and Kawamura folded his arms. It was such an odd reaction. What they'd said about Ryan was evident now—he had both of them completely cowed. Slater watched the three of them. He'd never seen a dynamic quite like this, and he'd never seen this side of Ryan.

Finally Marvel-Anne met his gaze and spoke quietly. "If you need to hear me say it, Ryan, I'm done."

"That makes no sense," Ryan said, waving an arm. "We've got work to do, and there's money to do it with. You love the search."

"I'm done," she said intently. "I need to move on."

Ryan gestured to Kawamura. "You're not done with him. How long have you been fucking him? That's such a skank move."

"You don't get to call me a skank," she said evenly.

"Him too," Ryan said, jutting his chin at Kawamura. "Archetypal skank. You lied to my face last night."

"So you caught me," Kawamura said, his voice calm. "You found Marvel-Anne, found us together. Mission accomplished. It doesn't change what we're doing. There's nothing more to say."

"You lied to me," he shouted. "Both of you."

"Of course I lied to you," Marvel-Anne said. "It was the only option. You would have found a way to pull us back into it."

"You're trying to do that now," Kawamura said. "But it's over. We're not going back into the forest."

Marvel-Anne gestured toward Slater. "Tell your goon to let us go."

"I'm not a goon," Slater said sharply. He stepped next to Ryan and put a hand on his shoulder. "But she's right. We have to go."

Ryan spun toward him, anger flashing in his eyes. "You too?"

Slater ignored that, and popped the magazine out of Kawamura's weapon, then deftly emptied the round from the chamber.

"This is a nice piece. Some of the cops carry these." He clicked the loose bullet into the mag, then tucked it in his back pocket, and set the empty gun on the kitchen island. He eyed Kawamura. "Nothing personal." To Ryan, he said, "Let's go."

"That's it?" Ryan demanded, throwing up his hands. "End of story? No more *Sasquatch Search*?"

"Hire someone else," Marvel-Anne said flatly.

"Sure," Ryan said, his voice breaking with emotion. "Like that'll be easy." Throwing both hands up over his head, he jabbed his index fingers at Marvel-Anne. "Fuck you," he shouted, then pointed to Kawamura. "And fuck you."

Kawamura gazed calmly at the table, and Marvel-Anne pursed her lips, but neither of them spoke. Slater put a hand on Ryan's back, and steered him toward the stairs. Ryan was still glaring at them, but he let himself be maneuvered.

"Bon voyage, assholes," he shouted, turning back to them.

Walking next to him, Slater guided him onto the stairs, and they started down. Ryan twisted around and shouted up at them, even though they were out of view.

"Traitors," he cried, and before Slater got him out the front door, he shouted once more: "Assassins."

Once they were on the street, Slater put an arm around his shoulder and led him toward the Thunderbird. Ryan's chest heaved with jagged sobs, and hot tears ran down his face.

Slater pulled open the passenger door for him, and put his palm on his head as he got in so that he wouldn't inadvertently bang it on the frame in his frazzled state. Slater slammed the door and then stepped across the street to the gutter, where there was a sewer grate. Glancing around to make sure he wasn't being observed, he pulled Kawamura's magazine out of his pocket, and wiped it off with his handkerchief, then stooped to drop it through the grate.

Climbing in behind the wheel, he didn't start the engine. Instead he sat there with Ryan, not watching him but listening to him cry. After a while his sobbing ebbed, and then subsided.

"After everything we built together," he said, his voice breaking.

"Looks like it's time to build something else."

"What, you're my analyst now?" he demanded.

Slater let it go, gazing out the windshield. Finally Ryan wiped his nose with the back of his hand and snorted, then took a deep breath.

"I guess this is it. What do I owe you?"

Slater thought about it, counting the days. "Another grand, plus five hundred in expenses."

"Expenses for what?" he said, pulling out his phone.

"I paid a guy to dig up those train tickets. He also found Kawamura's weapons license."

"It'll have to be electronic." He tapped at the screen. A moment later Slater felt a buzz in his pants as the funds landed.

"Why didn't you tell me you were going to the Natural History Museum?"

Ryan eyed him. "How do you know about that?"

"I thought you were playing me," Slater said. "I looked into what you were up to."

He scoffed. "So suspicious. It was bigfoot research."

"On the podcast you talk about nothing but bigfoot research. You kept this secret from me. Why was it different?"

"I guess I was embarrassed. This particular work strayed outside scientific orthodoxy. It involved paranormal channels."

"So it was psychic research. The liminal space between the real world and the metaphysical."

Ryan frowned. "That's correct."

Slater started the engine. "Where to?"

"I need to go to Portland," he said, and looked

at his phone.

"I'm not driving you there."

Ryan tapped at the screen. "There's a seat on a flight in two hours." He looked at Slater. "I need to get my stuff from your apartment. How long will it take to get from there to LAX in a ride-share?"

"I'll drive you," Slater said, and shifted into gear. "Book the seat. You'll make it."

As he accelerated down the freeway ramp, Ryan tucked his phone away and stared out the window.

"What are you going to do next?" Slater said. "In Portland?"

"What can I do? Recruit a new team, of course. It'll take a while to find the right people. They'll have to be open-minded, and savvy about the backwoods, and tuned in to preternatural stuff. The quest must go on. The importance of that is clearer to me now than ever before."

Slater glanced at him sidelong as he changed lanes, listening to his animated talk. Marvel-Anne's analogy of a cork in water was apt—it felt like Ryan was already on the rebound.

They rode in silence for a while, and then Ryan spoke, his tone serious.

"What about you and me?"

"We had some good times," Slater said, "but you said it last night. I'm not the guy for you."

Ryan frowned. "I said that?"

"I'm not surprised you don't remember. But I'm glad you figured it out. You're better off not worrying about me. I'm no damn good for people."

———◆———

INCHING THE THUNDERBIRD AROUND the upper loop at LAX, Slater pulled up to the curb, and he and Ryan both climbed out. Slater opened the trunk and pulled out the bulky backpack.

"I don't know how to thank you for your help," Ryan said, heaving it onto his shoulders.

He shrugged. "I got paid."

"Well, I had fun. All the sex, I mean."

"Take care of yourself. I'll be listening to the podcast."

Ryan stepped close and pulled him into a hug, then kissed him briefly on the mouth. He pulled away and stepped up onto the curb.

Slater climbed in behind the wheel, then eyed his side mirror and nosed into the traffic, catching a glimpse of Ryan in the rearview as he walked into the terminal, dwarfed by his big backpack. Whoever said "You should never meet your heroes" was on to something. The narrator would never sound the same to him again.

———◆———

Also from Dagmar Miura

That First Heady Burn

The first book in the Slater Ibáñez series sees Slater running surveillance on an injured tech worker and tangling with blackmailers, party girls, late-night hookups with a gamut of guys, and a lot of bourbon.

slater.dagmarmiura.com

Brawl in Bardo

Slater spends the night in a dusty Mojave Desert town and finds that things look different in the liminal space between LA and Vegas, like the bardo between lives. Soon he's stalking a sleazy dermatologist who's in a custody battle with another croaker for a seemingly worthless statue.

slater.dagmarmiura.com

The Mason Braithwaite Paranormal Mystery Series

No one is ever quite sure whether psychic investigator Mason gets results with actual psychic power or his more mundane flatfooting, but the disheveled redhead manages to resolve some intractable mysteries.

mason.dagmarmiura.com

Penstock Canyon

While helping out a friend suffering from late-night visitations, psychic investigator Mason is confronted with aliens on the roof and other liminal beings that have him questioning the very nature of reality.

mason.dagmarmiura.com

Truman and Celeste

Sometimes all a woman needs is a decent man—
even if she's not sleeping with him. Join Truman
and Celeste as they troll the gritty underbelly of
Los Angeles, never hesitating to slam that cocktail,
hit on guys, or ask the next relevant question.

truman.dagmarmiura.com

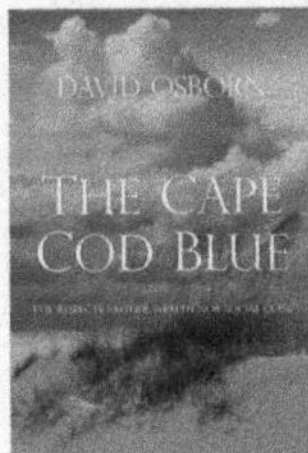

The Cape Cod Blue

The glittering, exalted world of art auctioning
hides love, hate, and parricidal murder in a
wealthy and socially prominent family when
forgery of an anonymous Cape Cod painting is
used to steal a world-famous portrait that's worth
a fortune.

capecod.dagmarmiura.com

The Bone Bridge

Yarrott Benz, the 2016 Ippy Award winner for
memoir, is forced to deal with extraordinary
self-sacrifice in this harrowing account of teenage
brothers, as different as night and day, trapped
together in a dramatic medical dilemma.

bonebridge.dagmarmiura.com

The Psychic Vegan Cookbook

It has never been easier to cook vegan, and you
don't even need to be psychic to do it. Whether
your motivation is eating healthier or the welfare
of other sentient creatures, Henrietta Flores
guides you through plant-based versions of familiar dishes.

cookbook.dagmarmiura.com

www.ingramcontent.com/pod-product-compliance
Lightning Source LLC
Chambersburg PA
CBHW010348170726
48284CB00011B/2830